SPY HIGH: MISSION FOUR

SPY HIGH:
MISSION FOUR

THE PARANOIA PLOT

A. J. BUTCHER

LITTLE, BROWN AND COMPANY
New York Boston

Based upon concepts devised by Ben Sharpe

Little, Brown and Company

Time Warner Book Group
1271 Avenue of the Americas, New York, NY 10020
Visit our Web site at www.lb-teens.com

First U.S. Edition 2004
First published in Great Britain in 2003 by Atom Books

Cover art by Jason Reed

ISBN 0-316-78879-1 (hc) / ISBN 0-316-76260-1 (pb)

10 9 8 7 6 5 4 3 2 1

Q-FF

Printed in the United States of America

PART ONE

CHAPTER ONE

There is a room with no windows, evenly lit by panels in the ceiling, in the walls, no way to distinguish night from day. A room beyond time. A room all in white, no identifying feature visible, like a man without a face. It could be anywhere.

A girl is sitting on a chair, her hands neatly folded in her lap, her eyes staring vacantly ahead, reflecting only whiteness, absence. The girl wears no clothes, but she doesn't seem to care. She doesn't seem to notice.

Neither does the man who smiles proudly at her from across the room. "You're looking well today, my dear," he says, like a doctor to a patient. "How are you feeling?"

The girl's mouth opens, and she tries to speak. No words come out, as though she is an actress who has forgotten her lines. A frown gathers at her forehead.

"It doesn't matter. It doesn't matter," soothes the man. "We'll try something else first. Stand up. Stand." He makes encouraging motions with his hands.

The girl looks down at her legs as if they have escaped her attention until now. She has two legs. They seem healthy. They seem strong. She leans forward on her chair and uses the muscles in her legs to lift her body upwards. Wobbling a little, uncertain like a baby, the girl stands.

The man applauds. "Well done. Oh, that's well done, my dear." Like he's praising a pet. "Now walk. To me. That's it." Beckoning with long fingers. "Walk to me."

The girl obeys, moves forward with the awkwardness of unfamiliarity. She is like a clockwork doll. She is like a man on the moon. She sways, and she lurches, and her arms dangle like a pendulum. But she gets there. With a low moan of effort in her throat, beads of sweat on her brow, she stands before the man.

He places his hands on her bare shoulders. Maybe she shudders, maybe she doesn't; it's hard to tell. "Well done, indeed," the man approves. "Now let's try some words. Tell me who you are. Tell me your name."

The girl's lips part as if eager to obey. Her jaw gyrates as if she's chewing toffee. "Uhh," she manages.

"Yes, I know," the man sympathizes. "Names are so difficult, aren't they, particularly one's own. Well, we'll try another, shall we? Who am I? What is *my* name?"

The girl frowns, shakes her head, defeated.

"Well, perhaps it doesn't matter just yet," the man smiles. "But what you'll do for me, my dear, that's what matters. So tell me that. What will you do for me?"

"Uhh . . . I . . ." With renewed determination. "An . . . ee . . ."

"Any," encourages the man. "Good. Excellent. You see? I knew you could do it. Keep going."

". . . th . . ." The girl struggles to please. She launches herself at the word like an artist on the high trapeze. ". . . thing . . ." She's got it.

"Thing," repeats the man, a smile unseaming his face like an opening wound.

"Anything . . . anything . . ." Like she's on automatic.

The man almost writhes with pleasure. "Oh, that is good,"

he delights. "That is well done, my dear." He almost wants to hug her. "Not long now and you'll be ready."

But ready for what he doesn't say.

"The submersibubble can descend to a depth of five hundred meters," informed the guide to the fascinated *oohs* and *aahs* of the morning's tourists. "The wide viewing ports around the circumference of the bubble are designed so that you don't miss a single detail of this beautiful underwater environment." Eager faces pressed against reinforced Plexiglas, gazed out at the coral and the multicolored fish flitting by. "Our aim is to bring you as close to our wonderful marine life as possible —" a brief pause — "without getting wet."

Everybody laughed. Everybody was feeling good.

Nelson Nolan laughed, too. To begin with. Until he realized something rather important, something he should perhaps have realized sooner.

Everybody else was laughing at *him*.

It was true. He glanced to his right. The woman there, she was pretending to be occupied by the viewing port, but she was laughing, she was making fun of him. And the impudent little boy on his left, he didn't even have the guile to turn away but met Nelson Nolan's inquiring stare directly, mouth flung wide in mockery.

Everybody. Everybody was laughing at him.

Nelson Nolan's neck whipped around. Ah, they were quick, the others. They'd snapped back to their own viewing ports, their own companions, just that fraction of a moment before he could catch them, that microsecond before he'd have seen them, all of them, watching him, sizing him up. Waiting.

He felt the buzzing again. The buzzing was back inside his skull, like a switch turned on, like a warning. The others. He wasn't going to turn his back on them now. He didn't dare. That would give them their chance.

What was that game he'd used to play as a child (when the other kids would let him play)? You faced a wall and everybody else crept up on you, stealthily, like murderers, like thieves, and you could turn around when you liked and if you saw someone moving that was all right, they were out, but if you didn't see anyone moving they were still in, they could still get you. And they were closer every time, closing in, surrounding you, stopping you breathing.

The buzzing in his head was louder now. He could hardly hear the guide speaking, even over the microphone.

". . . allows us to maintain a comfortable temperature inside the bubble whatever the depth . . ."

She was lying. It was warm in here, getting warmer. Nelson Nolan was sweating. There was sweat leaking thickly into his eyes like they were slowly drowning, but he didn't dare close them. If he shut his eyes, the others would be on him.

They wanted to do him harm. It was obvious. And they thought he couldn't get away, trapped with them in a bubble beneath the sea. No wonder they were biding their time. No wonder they were laughing at him.

A hand tugged at his sleeve. Nelson Nolan nearly screamed. It was the little boy. "Hey, mister, what fish is that? What kind of fish?" A ruse. A trick to distract his attention from the others. Nelson Nolan wasn't falling for it.

He struck the boy smartly across the cheek and leaped to his feet. "I know what you want!" he cried loudly, so he could hear himself above the buzzing. "You can't have me! I won't let you!"

Commotion now. The others realizing that they'd been rumbled. The boy bursting into bitter tears. Protesting adults standing. The guide, relentless cheerfulness briefly paused: "What's going on?" As if she didn't know.

His eyes darted in their sockets like hunted animals. He needed to defend himself. He needed a weapon. The others were circling him, toying with him. They'd learn. He spied a laser blade reserved for emergencies in a glass case above a fire extinguisher. They'd learn that Nelson Nolan was no easy prey.

Shouting, flailing his arms, he lunged for the blade. Smashed the glass, slicing his fingers. He didn't feel any pain, though. The buzzing in his brain blocked it all out. Energizing the laser blade, he whirled it around his head like the old-fashioned ax it had replaced. Heard screams, shrieks. Saw the others cringe from him.

He had to get out. He had to get out.

If only the buzzing would let him think.

The sealock. That was the ticket. That was the way out. The others would never follow him into the sealock. "You can't have me! No!" Exultantly.

He swung the laser blade, and his tormentors scattered. He was at the sealock door. He was punching the controls. "Stop him!" he heard, but nobody did.

The door was sliding open.

And his head was splitting now, as if the blade he held was burning, burrowing into it. But he was inside the sealock, and the inner door was closing, and it seemed a little cooler here, and that was good.

He was almost safe. He'd almost escaped. There was just one thin door remaining.

And the others weren't laughing at him anymore. He could see their faces, distorted in the sealock glass, lunatic and howling. They knew what he was about to do. They knew they'd lost him.

It was his turn to laugh now.

So Nelson Nolan did. He laughed as he activated the sealock's outer door. He laughed as the deep ocean waters crashed in upon him.

It was possible he was even laughing when the sea gushed into his mouth and into his nostrils and flooded his lungs. Possible, but not likely.

All the way out of the Border Zone, they were pursued by a procession of little Domer children, whooping and waving and pattering in old shoes as fast as they could to keep up with them. Here, evidently, SkyBikes were still a novelty, especially when ridden by people who were clearly outsiders. It was obvious even to the chasing children that the two teenagers so high above them, both blond and magnificent, the girl's long hair streaming behind her like a scarf, did not belong to the dome. Pop stars, was the general consensus afterward, or actor and actress shooting scenes for a movie. Nobody guessed they were secret agents in training.

"Aren't they sweet, Ben?" Lori Angel called across to her companion. He didn't appear convinced. "Go on, make their day and give them a wave." Her own arm could have belonged to a castaway signaling a rescue ship.

"You're doing well enough for both of us, Lo," Ben Stanton

replied huffily. "Spy High ever closes down and you've got a future as an aerobics instructor."

"A mid-aerobics instructor," joked Lori, pointing to the ground a neck-breaking distance below.

Ben didn't respond. He had more on his mind than a bit of banter or a crowd of Domer urchins with snotty noses and scuffed knees. The reason he and Lori were even here, squandering their holiday time when they could be basking on a beach somewhere or cruising on the Stanton family yacht, wasn't making him feel good for a start. Two words that had been a nagging problem for him throughout their first year at Deveraux Academy: Jake Daly.

The last time he'd seen Jake had been the end of term. A traumatic term. Jennifer's death had devastated them all, even himself, though as team leader he'd thought it best to try to put a brave face on things and look to the future. But Jake had been hurt worst of all. It was only to have been expected. Jennifer and Jake had been, well, involved, and if you lose someone you're that close to, you take a long time to recover. If you ever recover. The last time Ben had seen Jake, it didn't look like he would.

"I know it's hard, Jake," he'd said, "but these last few weeks, you just haven't been, well, not as sharp as you were before Jen . . . well, before."

"Is that right?" Jake hadn't taken the observation in the spirit in which it had been intended.

"I mean, next term we've got to try to get back to normal." He'd been thinking about the team. Operational effectiveness couldn't be compromised, even in the face of personal tragedy. It was in the manual.

"Is that right?" Jake's vocabulary had seemed even more limited than usual. "Well, listen to this." Angry, bitter. "I couldn't care less about next term. Right now, I couldn't care less whether I ever set eyes on Spy High or you again."

So it hadn't exactly been tearful farewells and promises to write. But now he was going to see him again.

Lori's idea, of course. "We can't take the risk that he means it, Ben." She'd said that. "We have to make sure that Jake comes back." She'd said that, too. "We'll have to persuade him. If necessary, we'll have to drag him back ourselves." Ben had wondered where she'd got the plural from. But reluctant as he might secretly have been, in that grudging part of himself that he never liked consciously to acknowledge, Ben couldn't let Lori pay a call on Jake alone. So here they both were, a week before the start of term, skimming through the air on their SkyBikes on a mission to keep what remained of Bond Team together.

"Cheer up, Ben," Lori was calling to him once more. "I thought you liked being the center of attention." Some children were still running after them, even though the Border Zone was falling behind and there seemed nothing ahead but fields and sky.

"Depends whose attention it is."

"Well, let's give you something to think about, shall we?" Lori reared up on her handlebars, clamped her knees to the bike's gleaming metal flanks, and opened the throttle wide. "I'll race you to Jake's farm. Loser had to milk the cows when we get there."

"Yeah?" Ben was always ready for a challenge. "Hope for their sake you've got warm hands."

"Ben," laughed Lori, "as if you didn't know!"

And she sped away from him then, accelerating toward the horizon and the distant glass arch of the dome. For a moment, Ben could only watch her go. For a moment, she was beyond him, out of his reach. She was already traveling so quickly, he felt he might lose her.

It was a feeling he didn't relish.

As it turned out, though, Ben had just about caught up with Lori by the time they swooped down to the Daly farm. "No fair," Lori complained. "You've been here before. I had to slow down to follow the navigator."

"Let's call it a draw," Ben declared magnanimously. "It'll save Jake's livestock a worrying experience."

The Dalys were there to meet them. Jake's parents, on day release from a Norman Rockwell painting. His little sister, Beth, trailing dolls from both hands and gawking at Lori in particular as if she'd recently witnessed a miracle. And Jake himself. Ben felt that he ought to be amused by the way Jake was dressed, in faded blue dungarees like some twenty-first century Huckleberry Finn, that he ought to make some quip about Jake only needing a straw of wheat to chew to complete the picture. But somehow Jake carried off the poverty of his clothing and the simplicity of his surroundings. There was a pride in him that could not be denied, a dignity, a strength. Ben didn't like to admit it, but he could see how girls might be attracted to Jake Daly — the tangle of black hair, the dark, magnetic eyes, the powerful body. There was something dangerous about Jake, and some girls liked danger. Fortunately, Ben reassured himself, Lori wasn't one of them. Even if she was throwing her arms around him and effusing about how good it was to see him. Lori was just a tactile sort of person.

"Jake," said Ben.

"Ben," said Jake.

They shook hands. Briefly.

Jake introduced Lori to his family. Mr. Daly's opinion was that she was "a real pretty girl," though his marriage was probably sound enough for Ben not to have to consider him as a rival. Little Beth on the other hand, certainly seemed to want Lori to herself.

"Are you really an angel?" she said wonderingly.

"No, honey," Lori smiled. "That's just my name. Like yours is Daly."

"Peggy and Glubb think you look like an angel." Beth thrust the two dolls under Lori's nose. Both had seen better days and had hopefully smelled better, too. "Peggy and Glubb think you've got an angel's hair."

"That's very nice of Peggy and Glubb to say so. My stylist will be pleased."

"Beth, sweetie," Jake suggested gently, "haven't you got a tea party to arrange?"

But the little girl was undeterred. "Peggy and Glubb have never been on a SkyBike. Not with an angel."

Ben knew what was coming next, and he wasn't wrong. Lori being Lori, offered to take Peggy and Glubb — and Beth, as it happened — for a ride on her SkyBike right there and then. And that was bad enough, leaving him alone with Jake and the senior Dalys. For obvious reasons, they couldn't talk about Spy High — not even their parents knew the real purpose of

Deveraux Academy — and farming as a topic of conversation for Ben was up there with stamp collecting and flower arranging as a viable alternative to watching paint dry. Worse still, though, little Beth was wanting big brother Jake to go with them, and big brother Jake was agreeing.

"Mind if I borrow your bike?" What could Ben say?

"We won't be long." From Lori by way of compensation.

You'd better not be, Ben thought, though somehow it came out as, "No, you take your time."

Lori smiled. Little Beth squealed. Jake had the temerity to wave as the SkyBikes lifted into the air. Ben watched them soar with a sinking heart. Mr. Daly was behind him: "Guess you'd like a look around the place. . . ."

Jake took them to the far field, where he'd once walked with Jennifer. He'd avoided coming here throughout the holidays so far, afraid of ghosts, maybe, but now, with Lori accompanying him, he felt it would be all right. Beth scampered off to play with her dolls, enabling Jake and Lori to talk freely.

"So what do you think of your first time in a dome?" Jake asked.

"Well . . ." Lori gazed up at the vast arc of steel and glass above her. She knew it was there for protection, to shelter the rich agricultural land from the ravages of the elements or from terrorist attacks (not that it had succeeded with the latter), to guarantee a healthy food supply for the nation. She knew its intentions were good. But it still looked like a prison to her. "Well . . ."

"Nice place to visit but wouldn't want to live here." Jake grinned without bitterness. "I know exactly what you mean."

"They've rebuilt it well, though, haven't they?" Lori looked for something positive to say. "After Nemesis . . ."

"You can't even see the cracks," Jake noted. "Everything back to normal. The crops growing. The farmers in their fields. A little less space in the cemetery, that's all."

"Jake," winced Lori.

"Sorry. Anyway, you might as well get to the point."

"Point?"

"Of your visit, Lo. When you videophoned me, saying you were coming, it was obvious you weren't just passing by and thought you'd call. Nobody ever just happens to be passing the domes. Certainly not Ben Stanton Jr. Bet he's loving this, isn't he?"

"This is Ben's idea, Jake," Lori lied unconvincingly. "He's worried about you. I'm worried about you." With greater sincerity. "We want to know what you're going to do, Jake. Are you coming back to us?"

"I thought so." Jake fixed his gaze beyond the eternity of rippling corn, the rhythms of nature that never changed. "You know, when Jennifer was killed, I thought that was it. Game over. No point anymore. Leave the secret agent stuff to people who cared. When I left Deveraux at the end of term, I really didn't expect to be going back. Thought maybe I'd please my old man and be a good honest farmer after all, just like he'd always wanted."

"But, Jake —"

"No, Lori. That was then. But coming back home, I've had time to think. Not too many distractions in the dome. And I've been thinking about Jennifer and all the others like her. Way too many others like her. The victims of the sickness out there, the terrorists and the lunatics and the guys who want to conquer

the world. Frankenstein. Nemesis. Talon. They're all gone now, but there'll be somebody or something else to take their place, won't there? That's the way it works. It's never over. You can win a battle, a lot of battles, but the war goes on forever. And thinking of Jen, I don't want that to happen to anyone else. No one else is going to die like that if I can do anything about it. No one." Jake's eyes glittered with purpose, his fists clenched. "Bottom line, Lo, I believe in Spy High now more than ever. So to answer your question, Am I coming back? Just try and stop me."

"Oh, Jake, I'm so glad." For the second time that day, Lori threw her arms around him. It was getting to be a habit.

Little Beth hooted with laughter as she saw it. "You've got to get married now!"

"One thing's for sure, anyway, Lo," grinned Jake. "This year can't be any worse than the last."

Elmore Grant, senior tutor at Deveraux Academy and former secret agent himself, peered at his own reflection in his bedroom mirror. The expression he saw was one of dismay. The gray hair looked grayer and, if anything, sparser. The lines on his face seemed deeper, like someone had been chiseling at them while he'd been asleep. Another year of school coming up. Another year of aging gracelessly all but over. Retirement, if not an immediate danger, was now featuring in his life like the mysterious masked enemy whose identity is revealed in the final chapter. Grant sighed, ran his hands through his hair automatically.

If only he could be young again.

He sat heavily on the edge of his bed, the way an old man sits. Thought back to the villains he'd battled in the past — evil men, madmen, even one or two who were women, and he'd beaten them all. He'd stood grand and tall — at least until he'd lost his legs. Why did time have to be the one foe he couldn't defeat?

But then, maybe there *was* a way.

His artificial limbs had given him a semblance of normality. When compared with real skin and bone, only a prosthetic surgeon would be able to tell the flesh from the fake. And there were further advances in cosmetic surgery of every kind by the day, it seemed. The future looked healthy. The future looked young.

So maybe there *was* a way.

He kept the card in his jacket pocket like a photograph of a lover, to be taken out and admired when no one else was looking. As he did now. A single address. A few simple sentences. A ridiculous hope. But they'd been positive before. They'd been pleased to see him, glad to help . . .

The sudden cannonade of the "1812 Overture" meant that someone was at the door. His driver, ready to escort him to Deveraux for the start of the term. He liked to start work a few days before the students arrived, and this year in particular, with the new member for Bond Team . . . well, not for the first time lately, Grant hoped that Jonathan Deveraux knew what he was doing. He hadn't agreed with the founder over this matter at all.

Maybe he was getting old.

A wry smile on his lips, Senior Tutor Elmore Grant went to answer the door. But it wasn't his driver who had come to take him to Spy High. Senior Tutor Elmore Grant couldn't actually believe who it was.

"It can't be," he breathed, backing away instinctively. "No . . ."

The figure at the door stepped inside. "Oh, but yes," it said. And it kept on coming.

It had always been the same for Lori. During the holidays, she could relegate school to the status of a distant memory or a dream, but as soon as school restarted, it was as if she'd never been away, and home and the holidays took their turn to seem unreal. She felt that way now, sitting in the rec room with the others sipping the first Coke of term, and all around her Deveraux Academy was exactly the same as ever. Its sprawling gothic-mansion disguise aboveground was as deceptive as the first day she'd seen it, while below, in secret rooms at the cutting edge of technological development, the training of the next generation of the espionage elite continued unabated. The true heart of Spy High beat on as if it would never stop.

Cally and Eddie hadn't changed, either. Her hair was still immaculately dreadlocked while his red mop still looked like it hadn't seen a comb since his twelfth birthday. Cally listened thoughtfully and intelligently to what everyone said; Eddie simply waited for the wisecracking opportunities to come along. But it was good that they were both here, Lori thought, with herself, Ben and Jake. Cally Cross and Eddie Nelligan were integral parts of Bond Team. Jennifer Chen had been the same. And of course, that was the change that couldn't be ignored, the only change that mattered. There was no Jennifer.

Eddie for one, though, seemed keen to avoid the subject. "You know, I nearly didn't come back, either," he said. "You're lucky to have me."

"Lucky's not exactly the word that springs to mind, Ed," said Ben.

"No, I mean it. It was a toss-up. I either came back to Spy High to lend my considerable wit and charm to the ongoing battle against global terror, or I stayed at home and continued to make the lives of the eligible females of my neighborhood worth living." Eddie shook his head self-sacrificingly. "In the end, I decided that saving the world was probably a little more important than a few broken hearts."

"We're honored, Eddie," said Cally. "Really."

"Yeah. Do any of these broken hearts have names?" Ben wondered, with what Eddie considered to be undue skepticism. Just because he and Lori had been an item virtually since day one. Other guys could get lucky once in awhile, too. He supposed.

"Of course they have names," he protested. There was a "such as?" in Ben's stare. "It's just that I don't think names are all that important. It's feelings that count."

"Well, you're partly right, Eddie." Jake's sudden intervention surprised his teammates. "And as usual, you're partly wrong. Feelings matter, yes, obviously, but so do names. Names are who we are. And there's one name nobody seems to want to mention: Jennifer."

"Jake," said Cally, "we thought —"

"No, it's fine, Cal. Really. That's what I want to say now so we can move on. Jen's gone. I know it. I'm living with it. And maybe I'd sooner we did talk about her. Otherwise, it's a bit like Jen's just been forgotten."

"We'll never forget her, Jake," Cally promised.

"Cal's right," said Eddie. "So what I'd like to know is what's next. For us, I mean. Bond Team. Do we stay as five this year, or do we get a new member to take us back up to the regulation six?"

The question had been preying on Ben's mind as well. "Maybe Grant'll tell us," he opined. "Maybe that's why he wants to see us in his study in about —" consulting his watch — "about now, actually."

"Best to make a move, then," said Eddie.

"You're in a hurry." Jake's eyes narrowed suspiciously. "You expecting something?"

"Just don't want to start term with a black mark for punctuality, that's all," said Eddie, sounding hurt. Of course, if they *were* having a new member, and if that new teammate *did* happen to be female and gorgeous and probably in need of an experienced hand (with other body parts available on request) to show her around, then Eddie felt it was his duty to be first in line to offer his services.

And it looked like his luck might well be in effect.

After the usual pleasantries, Grant became more serious, talked about the sad loss of Jennifer but how the school, while still mourning her, had to move on, and how Mr. Deveraux in his wisdom had decided that a new student should join Bond Team as of today and how she — *she* — was going to be here to be introduced to her teammates any minute now. Eddie began to wish he'd combed his hair after all. And maybe brushed his teeth as well.

"Her name is Rebecca Dee," said Grant.

(Coincidentally, Rebecca had always been Eddie's favorite girl's name, and Dee was pretty high on his list of great last names, too.)

"Can I ask whether this Rebecca's skill levels are on par with a second year team," Ben was saying, "or will she need extra training?"

"All in good time, Ben," said Grant.

Yeah, Ben, thought Eddie. *Who cared what her skills were like as long as she looked good in a shock suit?* Stanton had no sense of priorities. "We'll make sure Rebecca fits in, sir," he added nobly.

"I'm sure you will, Eddie," Grant acknowledged as a knock came at the door. "And here's your chance to start. This must be her now. Come in."

These were Bond Team's thoughts as the door opened, and someone they'd never met before but who could well mean life or death to them on future missions entered, and they saw her for the first time. Ben: *Let her be good, but not too good.* Jake: *Whatever she's like, she'll never replace Jen.* Lori: *I'm sure we'll be the best of friends.* Cally: *I feel safer with people I trust.* Eddie: *Please, God, let her be The One, or at least in the ballpark.*

The girl stepped into the study. Not tentatively. Not nervously. Boldly. Confidently. With a stud in her nose and a rash of piercings in both ears. With short, spiky hair, green. With a lot of makeup, also green. Wearing clothes that looked like they'd been stolen en route from the street. Who smiled broadly at Grant and the assembled teenagers. "You all been waiting for me? Hey, hope I'm not a disappointment."

"Bond Team," said Grant, "this is Rebecca Dee."

"Ah, not quite." The girl raised a green-nailed finger. "Sorry to correct you on my first day, Mr. Grant, sir, but it's not Rebecca. It's Bex. Bex Dee. And I just know from now on things are gonna be wild."

"Thank you, Lord," said Eddie.

CHAPTER TWO

IGC DATA FILE GRT 3140

. . . ahead of the final completion of the Guardian Star. The permanently manned space station has been a pet project of the president since before his election, and will now form the first line of defense in America's Earth Protection Initiative (EPI). The Guardian Star's weaponry, sufficient to reduce an average-size country to ashes in a matter of hours, will be directed toward the distant stars, forever alert to possible incursions by alien forces from the vastness of space.

"Those boys out there may be friendly," President Westwood said, "and if they are, they'll find that we earthlings'll welcome them with open arms. But if any extraterrestrial types come a-visiting and they turn out to be hostile, then they need to know and need to know fast that this great planet of ours is not one to take liberties with and that we can defend ourselves if need be. EPI and the Guardian Star in particular are just part of that defensive capability, and I'm really proud of what we've achieved in such a short time."

Not everyone, however, seemed to share the president's enthusiasm. Democratic Senator Al Nathanson went on record recently to claim that the billions of dollars devoted to EPI constituted "the greatest waste of money in the history of the United States." Senator Nathanson went on to say that there was no proof as yet that life even existed on other planets, making preparations for an attack rather premature. "All those guns and missiles, all that destructive power," he added, "at the moment it's all pointing outward, and that's okay. But what's making me lose sleep is what happens if someone decides to turn the Guardian Star around by 180 degrees and sets its sights on Earth. What do we do then?"

Supporters of EPI have accused Senator Nathanson of scaremongering.

"The Guardian Star is watching over us all," a White House spokesperson said, "and keeping us safe."

It is rumored that President Westwood himself may even visit the space station to mark the beginning of this new era. . . .

"So, Rebecca . . ."

"Uh-uh, Ben," came the correction, "it's not Rebecca. It's Bex."

"Whatever you say." Ben didn't enjoy being put right on anything. "So, *Bex,* as you're one of the team now, what about telling us something about yourself."

They'd left Grant's study and returned to the rec room. One or two of the other students had already glanced curiously at the new girl with Bond Team. Simon Macey, leader of arch rival Solo Team and Ben's personal choice as the one he'd most like to see spontaneously combust, had not only glanced curiously at Bex but burst into laughter as well. Ben didn't approve of anything that allowed Macey to mock him. Studs and piercings did not appear on the Stanton list of acceptable fashion accessories, either.

If Bex Dee cared, though, she wasn't showing it. "Something about myself?" She seemed to consider. "Isn't much to tell, actually. I don't want to bore you all senselessly less than an hour into our acquaintance. Besides, I think a little bit of mystery's good for the soul, don't you?"

"Absolutely," Eddie agreed vigorously. He happened to be sitting very close to Bex.

"It's a mystery how Eddie ever got to Spy High in the first place, isn't it?" Cally joked.

"No, but what about you, Bex?" Ben pressed. "How come you're being put straight in with us second years, us final year students, and not starting with the first years?"

"Oh, I've done the same training you have," Bex said, "only at another Deveraux facility."

Everyone was surprised at that. "I didn't know there was another Deveraux facility," said Lori.

"Oh, sure." Bex was casual. "Only this one's kind of like for Spy High reserves. We were students on the shortlist for the A-Team, but we weren't thought to be quite ready when the final selections were made. So they bundled us off to a substitute school, and we trained, and we learned, and we lived in hope that somebody here dropped out or got mind-wiped or something so we could take their place. Kind of like a promotion. You could say this is my big break."

"Good for you," praised Jake sarcastically. "It makes Jennifer's death so worthwhile."

"That's uncalled for, Jake," said Eddie.

Bex regarded Jake directly, met his gaze, and did not look away. "I heard about Jennifer. I know I never knew her, but I'm sorry. Really. I'd sooner have stayed with the subs than get here because of that. But we can't change the past. Believe me, I know. We can only forge the future. And I'm here now. I'm one of you. And believe me, I want to make this work. Okay?"

Jake nodded, if only slightly. "You've got it," he said, "Bex."

"Excellent," enthused Eddie. "Now how about I show you around, Bex? Give you the grand tour kind of thing. You know, just you and me. The others'd come, too, but just before you arrived, they were saying they had loads of things to do, isn't that right, guys?"

"Just a minute, Eddie," Ben cautioned. "I'm not sure we —"

"Ben, we're training to be spies, not playing on Twenty Questions. Let's leave the interrogations for when we get captured by the bad guys, yeah?" Eddie ushered an amused Bex from the table. "If we get lost, don't come looking for us."

"Watch yourself, Bex," warned Cally. "Eddie's more dangerous than he looks."

"He'd have to be," grinned Bex. "See you all later. I hope."

They watched Eddie and Bex leave the rec room. "Looks like Eddie's taken a shine to our newest teammate," Lori said.

"Yeah? What about the rest of you?" Ben seemed skeptical.

"Meaning?" prompted Jake.

"Meaning there's something about her that I don't entirely trust."

"Come on, Ben," said Cally, "just because Bex is clearly not from your side of the street doesn't automatically make her an enemy mole or something. So she's got green hair and a few piercings. What? You think they're bugs, maybe? Cut the girl some slack."

"I agree with Cal, Ben," Lori said reluctantly. "Bex has been selected by the same people who chose us. We have to assume she's legit."

"Girls with a bit of spirit get you flustered, leader man?" Jake needled.

"All right, all right." Ben conceded defeat, raised his hands. "I get the message. We've got nothing to worry about. But —" he glanced thoughtfully toward the door — "maybe Eddie'll learn a little more about Miss. Rebecca Dee."

In the hologym observation room, Eddie was certainly giving it his best shot. "So why green, though? I mean, it's really good and all, stands out . . ."

"Well, I love nature, Eddie," Bex said dreamily. "I think growing things are a real turn-on, don't you?"

"I know what you mean. I nearly dated a pot plant once."

"And green's the color of nature, isn't it? So by dyeing my hair green . . ."

"You're like, communing with nature, right?"

"Wrong. I'm lying, you idiot." Bex laughed. "Green's today. I might be blue tomorrow. It's random. It's whatever I feel. There's no big idea."

Eddie laughed, too, to hide his blush. "I knew that. Course I did. Just playing along, that's all."

"Really? Bet you're great undercover." Bex looked at her watch, suddenly seemed restless. "So is that it for the tour?"

"There's Training Chamber Four still," said Eddie hopefully.

"Excellent, but if it's the same as Training Chambers One, Two, and Three only with a bigger number, I'm betting we can skip it."

"Maybe," Eddie had to admit. The tour was over, to be fair. The training chambers, the virtual reality chamber and the cyber-cradles, the Intelligence Gathering Center, the Gun Room, the Hall of Heroes, the computer suites, every last classroom and study area in Spy High — Eddie had escorted Bex around them all. And he would have been more than happy to repeat the same process again if it meant he and Bex would get to spend more time together. "But did I tell you about how no one's seen Mr. Deveraux in the flesh since they've been here, how he lives in his rooms and never —"

"Cut. Cut." Bex was not impressed. "I know about Mr. Deveraux, Eddie. In our line of training, who doesn't?"

"Well, we could go back and talk some more with old Violet at reception . . ." He was desperate now. Actively suggesting conversation with cranky old Crabtree, he had to be.

"I don't think so," Bex said. "What was it, Mrs. Crabtree said? 'Standards must be slipping? In my days girls with ironmongery in their nostrils wouldn't have gotten through the front door'? What does she know, the decrepit old biddy, ex–secret agent or not — I've got as much right to be here as anyone, maybe more. No, Eddie, thanks for the offer, but I think I'll head to my room, settle in a bit with Lori and Cally."

"You want me to come with you?" From out of the jaws of defeat, Eddie still hoped to snatch victory.

"No need. I think I can make it." She peeked again at her watch, smiled expansively at Eddie. "We're going to get along, aren't we?"

"Oh, yes." It was difficult to say more with your tongue hanging out.

Bex squeezed Eddie's hand. "See you later," she said. She winked. She left.

How much later? Eddie wanted to know. He even followed Bex out of the observation room to ask her precisely that question, but she'd already vanished from sight, obviously eager to get back to Lori and Cally. Maybe to talk to them about him, Eddie thought.

He might have changed his mind if he could have seen Bex just then, however, her lips set, her expression cold. She was certainly eager to get somewhere, but not, at least to begin with, to her own room.

* * *

In another room, a room with no windows, a girl sits on a chair and stares into space. Her chest rises and falls as she breathes, but otherwise, she exhibits no sign of life.

A man stands behind her and strokes her hair tenderly, almost lovingly, like a father with a favorite child. "Ah, you're coming along so well, my dear," he croons. "You've already made such progress. All the sacrifices, all the struggles have been worthwhile." The girl could be inclining her head in agreement, or maybe she just wants to escape the feel of his fingers? "I know how you've suffered, I know your pain, but you need be patient only a short time longer. The suffering will soon be theirs and you will be free of them at last." The man chuckles affectionately. He has sheafs of something in his free hand. "Let me remind you."

Photographs flutter like dead birds onto her lap, cold against her skin. The girl shivers. Her fingers tremble as she takes hold of the photographs and looks at them. Five of them. Five smiling faces, faces that have never seen the room with no windows.

The first: a girl, beautiful, blond, blue eyes sparkling with life and hope.

A change in her breathing. Faster. Fearful.

The second: a redheaded boy laughing almost aloud as if the girl whom his silver nitrate eyes cannot see is a fine joke.

Her eyelids fluttering. Her lips twitching.

Third and fourth: a black girl, a blond boy, conspiring together against her, united against her.

A low moan in her throat, hands plucking at the photographs.

"That's it," encourages the man. "Express yourself. You know you want to."

And the fifth photograph: a dark, moodily attractive boy, mocking her with his strength and his vitality.

Her shaking fingers tear at the photographs, pulling them apart.

And the man is rubbing his hands together, bobbing his head in pleasure. Laughing loudly as shreds of faces fall to the floor.

That first week, Ben kept a close eye on Bex. If the others wanted to accept a stranger into their midst without question or qualm, that was their right. But he was burdened with the responsibilities of leadership, and leaders had to be alert to any possible danger from any possible source. All right, so maybe Bex wasn't likely to turn out to be Stromfeld's daughter or something, but if she wasn't up to scratch, if she didn't gel with the team in crisis situations, Ben considered that to be sufficient grounds for removal. There could be no weak link at Spy High. Weak links reserved you a place next to Jennifer in the Hall of Heroes with holographic immortality and talk of noble sacrifice. Ben intended to retire gracefully.

So he watched Bex like a teacher grading a student, and his report was not favorable. History of Espionage with Grant: limited knowledge, but an inability to remember the founding members of M17 was not likely to prejudice your survival in anything but the end of term quiz. Spycraft: weak, and more worrying, as techniques that worked for the greats in the past would probably be successful again now. Weapons Instruction with the luscious Lacey Bannon: hopeless — she could hardly tell one end of a shock blaster from another, and as for accuracy of shooting, they might have to introduce barn doors for targets if they wanted Bex to hit anything. Martial Arts with Mr. Korita: Ben had to concede that Bex looked the part in a *judogi* and left it at that. In all areas of their training, she was making even Eddie appear expert. For Ben, however, the decisive moment came with the Space-Spheres.

Corporal Keene explained their purpose. "The spheres are a self-contained life-support system for agents engaging in espionage activities beyond the Earth's atmosphere."

"As you do," said Eddie.

"Nelligan," barked Keene, "sadly a Space-Sphere could well save your life one day, so I suggest a little more attention and a little less trying to play footsie with Dee."

"Yes, sir. Sorry, sir."

Keene circled the sphere that was before them. It resembled a bubble, but a bubble large enough for someone to stand inside and not have to stoop. Like a bubble, it was entirely transparent, permitting Bond Team an unobstructed view of its innards: self-securing stirrups for the feet and gauntlets for the hands. Suspended from the skin of the sphere was a harness for the upper body so that even if the stabilizing mechanism failed or was damaged in combat, the occupant would retain his or her balance and therefore his or her operational effectiveness. Multicolored strands of wire hung from a metal plate inlaid into the sphere above where an occupant would stand, like veins in an anatomical drawing. "Notice the adhesive patches on the end of each wire," Keene pointed out. "These will be taped to the forehead of whoever is operating the sphere. That operator will then be able to access and direct the sphere's guidance and defense systems by the power of thought alone, increasing significantly their ability to respond swiftly to any developments that might endanger the successful completion of the mission."

"Assuming the operator can think," whispered Cally to Lori, possibly with Eddie in mind.

"The outer skin of the sphere itself appears solid," continued Keene, "but the material is in fact extremely ductile." To prove the point, he pressed his hand against the bubble's side. It sank in. "This property helps to preserve the integrity of the sphere and will allow it to mold itself to the airlock door of any spacecraft its operator wishes to infiltrate. Each sphere is equipped with a mechanism guaranteed to override any airlock's entry codes."

"So have I got this right?" Bex asked, with what Ben interestedly interpreted as a gulp. "If we ever get to use these things, we kind of bail out of a spaceship like parachutists, and we pilot them through space using sort of telepathy, and then we stick like limpets to another spaceship and just kind of clamber inside."

"Dee," said Keene, "small wonder you're here."

"So do we get a trial run, Corporal?" Ben hoped, slyly observing Bex's reaction. He wasn't surprised to register her dismay, but it still didn't exactly inspire confidence.

"Training Chamber Four," directed Keene. Which was huge, vaster than the other training chambers put together, and which was plunged right now, apart from minimal lighting on the platform just below the ceiling where Bond Team and Corporal Keene stood, into total, absolute darkness. Like outer space without the stars, and probably not a coincidence.

"Saving on the electricity bill, sir?" said Eddie.

"Into a sphere, Nelligan," Keene responded gruffly, "and try saving your breath instead."

There was a Space-Sphere provided for each student. Bond Team pulled the skin of the spheres open, like pulpy, plastic curtains, and stepped through, quickly adopting the correct operational position. Harness attached. Stirrups and gauntlets engaged. Psi-wires pressed to the temples. The spheres lit up as the student's minds activated them, warm and yellow in the frosty darkness.

"Now let's see you fly!" ordered Keene. "Plenty of room out there." He indicated the yawning pit that was Training Chamber Four.

"Yeah, but Corporal Keene, sir," Eddie ventured, "what happens if we fall?"

"You fall here," returned Keene, "you get a nice soft landing on an air-mat. You fall from space, you get burned to a crisp reentering the atmosphere."

"Best not to fall, then," Eddie concluded lamely.

Ben could see that Cally, for one, wasn't going to fall. Her sphere was already lifting gently and smoothly from the platform, floating out beyond the security of solid steel into the void. It seemed effortless. Cally was laughing at the ridiculous pleasure of it. But then, Cally seemed sometimes more at home with computers than with people, more likely to date a laptop than a boy. She was a natural for telepathic communion with a Space-Sphere. Not that it was too hard. Ben joined Jake, Lori and even Eddie in trembling their spheres into movement, into life, more jerkily than Cally, maybe, but steadily, confidently.

Only Bex was finding the process difficult. Ben could see her shaking her head and frowning, like she was resisting the moment of interface between her mind and the cyber-brain of the sphere. She wasn't allowing herself to relax, to become one with her vehicle.

The others were now bobbing in the black like buoys on a midnight sea.

"Dee!" yelled Keene. "What are you waiting for, the end of the world? Get out there before I boot you out there!"

Cally was growing adventurous, swooping and circling in the darkness like a kite with no strings. "This is amazing!" she was crying. Everyone but Ben was watching her, admiring her skills.

So only Ben saw what happened to Bex, saw her sphere lurch into life like a car started by a learner, saw it tip over the edge of the platform like off the brink of a cliff. It was Bex's choice at that point. She could do what she was in the team to do, she could focus, she could concentrate, she could fly; or she could reject her responsibilities and give in to gravity and fall. Ben saw her close her eyes. He heard her scream.

Bex plummeted to the air-mat an unknown distance below.

Her scream was still in his ears later, on his way to Grant's study. As were the sympathetic rationalizations of his teammates: Don't worry about it, Bex. . . . It's difficult. . . . We did psi-training last year. . . . You'll get the hang of it. . . . I'm happy to offer some personal tuition, Bex. . . . All excuses. All misguided. *This time,* Ben thought, *Rebecca Dee fell on her own. Next time, who was to say she wouldn't take the whole team with her?* He was Benjamin T. Stanton Jr. He wasn't about to let any incompetent newcomer drag him down.

"So really, sir," he explained to Grant, "given the poor quality of her performances so far, I believe that Rebecca poses a serious threat to the operational effectiveness of my team. I don't think we can justify keeping her on. I'm sorry for her, obviously, but . . ." Ben shrugged his shoulders in a what-can-I-do sort of way.

"I expected this," Grant said from behind his desk, "sooner or later."

"That Rebecca wouldn't be up to it?" Ben assumed.

"No. That you'd come to me complaining about her." Grant leaned forward. His gray hair looked glossier today. Maybe he was treating it with something. "You like to be in control, don't you, Ben? You like everything neat, tidy, and ordered. I didn't expect you to relish change."

"It's not that, sir," Ben defended himself. "It's just that as team leader —"

"As team leader, it's your responsibility to look after the welfare of your team," Grant pointed out, a little confrontationally, Ben thought, a little unlike the senior tutor's usual, more diplomatic style. "It is not your responsibility to choose its members. That is mine."

"Yes, sir." Ben knew when to exercise the better part of valor.

"If Rebecca Dee is finding any part of her training at Spy High something of an obstacle, it is your duty to help her overcome that obstacle."

"Yes, sir."

"Leadership is not simply about taking the credit for success, Ben. It's about taking steps to prevent failure."

"Of course, sir."

"If Rebecca Dee is a problem, I suggest you solve it."

And Ben found himself back outside Grant's study door, lectured, admonished, and not happy. Who was Grant to talk to him like that? Senior tutor of Spy High, that was who, second only to Jonathan Deveraux himself. Ben could have kicked himself. He'd gone to Grant in good faith, to raise a genuine issue, and he'd only succeeded in turning the spotlight from Bex's abilities as a student to his own performance as team leader. He was beginning to wish he'd never set eyes on Rebecca Dee. Maybe she'd catch an infection from one of her piercings or something, and he'd get rid of her that way.

He needed to be cheered up, which meant one of two choices: Lori or the Sherlock Shield display in the Hall of Heroes. Since the irritation had more to do with Spy High than his personal life, Ben opted for the latter. Past successes always made him feel better about the future.

He took the nearest study elevator below ground, reentered the school proper. In the Hall of Heroes, there were two kinds of memorial: one commemorating the dead, the other celebrating the feats of the living. Prominent among these were holographic representations of the teams that had won the Sherlock Shield, the prize for victory in the first year inter-team competition at Deveraux. Last year, Bond Team had triumphed. Ben liked to go and look at himself sometimes, and dream of further glories to come.

Today, though, he didn't get as far as the Sherlock Shield display. As soon as he saw Lori and Jake together, he kind of changed his mind. Lori and Jake. Together. Ben stepped smartly backward and out into the corridor so that they wouldn't notice him. They certainly hadn't been aware of him. Their backs were to him. They were standing before the hologram of Jennifer, and Jake's head was kind of hanging forward, and Ben could see that his fists were clenched. Lori was close to him, her body pressing against his, and, as Ben watched, she eased a slender arm around his shoulders (the way she did with him). As though she'd waited for Ben's arrival before she did it. . . . She was talking to Jake quietly, earnestly, but Ben was too far away to hear what she was saying.

Not that he wanted to, anyway. It might be incriminating. Lori's arm. Around Jake's shoulders. Ben turned back the way he'd come.

He was not having a good day.

IGC DATA FILE GRT 3276

". . . and then she made us all kneel on the floor and put our hands on our heads," Ms. Boone continued, "and we all did it. I mean, when somebody comes into work wrapped in explosives and points a laser rifle at you point-blank you kind of listen to what they're saying, right? But I still didn't think we were in any real danger from her, not Mary Bannon. I mean, some of us had worked with her for years. She'd always been so normal, so dull if you really want to know. No man in her life. Maybe that was it.

"So anyway, then she starts getting anxious and going on about the enemies and how the enemies are among us and they mean to destroy us and how they think we can't tell the good people from the enemies but they're wrong, she said. It's green eyes, she said. Green eyes give them away. And she said it was her duty to remove anyone with green eyes for the sake of us all.

"Now that got Paul Dolfuss from accounts really sweating, 'cause not only does he have green eyes but he was on the end of the line nearest Mary Bannon, and she was looking at him and shouting, 'Green eyes!' and he tried to get out of it, and I heard him sobbing that he'd retincture his eyes to any color she liked so long as she let him live. It didn't look likely. Mary Bannon told him to stop blubbering and stay where he was, or she'd shoot him then and there.

"And she was coming down the line, and we were all screaming though my eyes are brown so I thought as long as Mary Bannon was consistent and the light in the office was good enough, I'd probably be all right. Same wasn't true for poor Millicent Phillips, however. Eyes green as grass. So she rammed her eyelids shut, and she was crying, 'They're blue! They're blue! They're off-green!' but Mary Bannon wasn't convinced and she stuck her fingers in Millicent's eyes and peeled back her eyelids like wrapping paper and Millicent's squealing but her eyes are still green so Mary Bannon shoves her over toward Paul Dolfuss.

"Then I'm realizing she's right in front of me, and we're gazing into each other's eyes, and she's smiling the way mad people smile, and she tells me, 'Brown eyes, Stacey. Very good. You're not an enemy. You can go.' And then I notice something. Mary Bannon's own eyes. Her own eyes are green. And when I tell her so, she doesn't believe me. So someone gives her a little mirror, and when she looks at herself and realizes it's true, she kind of wails and throws the mirror away, and it shatters. And the last thing she said was 'Green eyes! That's how you can tell! I'm one of the enemies!' And then, before anyone could stop her, not that anyone was gong to, she just kind of drops the laser rifle and hurtles down the corridor and into one of the other offices and slams the door behind her. Like she's running away from someone. But you can't run away from yourself, can you? And the rest of us are on our feet and thinking quick getaways but Millicent Phillips says, 'What if Mary comes back?'

"And that's when we hear the explosion from down the corridor. And that's when we know that Mary Bannon isn't coming back. I'm telling you, I know we live in a dangerous world, but I've never seen anything like . . ."

* * *

"Are you okay, Ben?" Touching him lightly on the arm, Lori seemed concerned.

"Sure. Any reason why I shouldn't be?" He tried not to sound aggressive.

Lori smiled reassuringly. "It's all right. I know what's bothering you. But you don't need to worry. I'm sure Bex is going to work out just fine."

Only half a diagnosis, Dr. Angel, thought Ben. It was how she and Jake were working out that was also on his mind. Maybe he should just come right out and ask her. There had to be nothing to it. He was being paranoid. Lori wasn't the cheating type, even if he didn't trust Daly not to take advantage of her good nature. But Corporal Keene was already calling them together for their SkyBike practice. Personal matters would have to wait.

An obstacle course had been set up in the extensive grounds to the rear of Deveraux Academy, with the operative word being "up." The obstacles, an assortment of poles, bars, hurdles, and hoops, hovered in the air about thirty meters above the ground. Keene controlled their height and position from a laptop. "Designed to test your maneuverability," he was explaining. "SkyBiking is not simply about speed. Now, who wants to play guinea pig?"

"I've always had a thing for little furry animals, Corporal Keene, sir," piped up Eddie, "and I'm a great mover."

"Very well, Nelligan," sighed Keene. "Let's see what you can do."

"Yes!" Eddie punched the air confidently. If there was one

area of their training that he instinctively excelled at, it was SkyBiking. Vehicles were to Eddie what computers were to Cally. He grinned at Bex, tipped her a wink.

"Something in your eye, Ed?" Jake wondered.

Eddie ignored him, mounted his bike. At last, a chance to really impress Bex. He activated the magnetic engine and took to the skies. He'd be more than a match for any course set by Keene.

"Hey, what about some encouraging cheers?" he yelled down to his teammates. "Some light applause?"

"Get on with it, Nelligan!" snapped Keene. "We haven't got all day!"

"Thought you said it wasn't all about speed, sir," called Eddie, "but if time is pressing . . ."

He accelerated suddenly and startlingly, streaking toward the waiting obstacles.

If they were honest, Eddie's teammates and even Corporal Keene would have had to admit that he was pretty impressive. At a blurring speed, he zipped between poles and through hoops, angling the SkyBike impeccably to negotiate the course, like a master skier tackling the Olympic slalom. His movements were fluid, liquid, human and machine in breathtaking harmony.

"Is this the same Eddie as yesterday or a different one?" Bex asked Cally.

"There's only one Eddie," Cally said.

He was arcing now to make his return run. And maybe he shouldn't have waved just then, an extravagant gesture, no doubt for Bex's sake. Maybe the others would have recognized the truth sooner. Though it probably wouldn't have made any difference if they had.

Eddie's SkyBike shot off so quickly, he toppled backward and almost fell. "What's going on? What's he trying to do?" Lori laughed. Eddie clowning about as always.

It happened suddenly, as if the bike was alive and determined to throw its rider. It reared and plunged, veering dramatically from side to side. Eddie seemed to be holding on for dear life. It all looked more than faintly ludicrous.

"What do you think you're doing, Nelligan?" raged Keene. As the SkyBike charged drunkenly into the obstacles.

"I see what you mean, Cally," grinned Bex. "Same old Eddie. What a joker."

Cally, however, was not grinning. As Eddie ducked low to avoid one bar that threatened to decapitate him, and as another pole cracked painfully against his leg. "This isn't a joke," she realized. "I don't know how, but Eddie's in trouble." She looked for confirmation from the others. No laughter now. The danger was dawning on all of them. "His SkyBike's out of control."

CHAPTER THREE

Typical, was the thought that flitted across Eddie's mind. How come Ben or Jake never find themselves in situations like this? How come imminent disaster only had a season ticket for Eddie Nelligan? Whatever happened to the luck of the Irish?

Eddie gripped the handlebars fiercely as the bike bucked and swerved. At least the obstacles were falling harmlessly to the ground now. Keene must have deactivated them. Pity he couldn't do the same for this insane SkyBike, but down below both teacher and teammates were limited to running after him and yelling advice that he couldn't hear. Up here, Eddie was on his own — just him and a hunk of murderous metal.

Wrapping one arm around a handlebar so tightly he felt his shoulder almost dislocate, Eddie dared to use his other hand to punch in what he hoped were the manual systems override codes on the SkyBike's control panel. Either they weren't, or the wretched machine was refusing to obey. Instead, it seemed to increase its speed, the rushing stinging Eddie's skin, blinding his eyes. The bike was like a rocket, like a missile, moving toward collision with the hard earth.

So Eddie had a new priority. He doubted he'd be able to impress Bex with his limbs in plaster or from a hospital bed (or even with a front row seat at his funeral). Best to stay aloft, maintain height, and try to devise some sort of plan. Equipping SkyBikes with parachutes in the future might be of help.

It was going to be difficult. Eddie was straining on the handlebars with strength he didn't know he had, gritting his teeth, wanting to yell. But the machine was resisting him, apparently determined on self-destruction. Eddie was holding his own at the moment, keeping the bike from dropping, but that wouldn't last. He had the messy vision of his biceps bursting and his muscles dribbling out from his sleeves just as he hit the ground and went splat.

So what about that plan?

The others were way behind now. The open ground was gone. He was skimming above part of the forest, and not sufficiently far above it for his liking, either. The treetops plucked for his feet like eager fingers. Much lower at this velocity, and they'd have his legs off at the knees.

Plan, plan, plan. Ben would have come up with something by now. But him, he was out of his . . .

Got it. Depth. Got it.

The lake. On the far side of the trees. The big, wet, *liquid* lake. Plunging in from this height, it'd still be like striking concrete, but at least there was a chance of survival — a good chance if Eddie got his timing right.

The trees fell away and the lake took their place, blue and inviting. His first stroke of good fortune: The bike's trajectory was taking him directly across it. Now, if he suddenly pressed down on the handlebars instead of up . . .

Eddie cried out as the SkyBike pitched into a wild, reeling descent. The air was screaming, too, as the lake spun dazzlingly, dizzyingly toward him. He let go of the handlebars, felt himself almost snatched from the saddle. The bike hurtled ahead of him. The sky somersaulted like a gymnast.

Relax that body. Hold that breath. Here comes impact.

The water rammed into Eddie like a rock. Total blackness.

Hold on to that consciousness like you did to the handlebars. Let it go, and *you're* gone. Hold that breath. Crystal eruptions of light above your head. Strike for the surface.

He surged into the clean air, gasping and spluttering. His body felt like it was burning with pain, but he could also feel that no major damage had been done. He'd live.

Eddie swam toward the bank to wait for the others to come and get him. He wondered what Bex's thinking was regarding trainee secret agents who narrowly cheated almost-certain death. It had to be a turn-on, didn't it? Maybe there was something in the luck of the Irish after all.

IGC DATA FILE GRT 3280

. . . protests continue to grow as the Guardian Star prepares to enter active service. A vigil is being kept outside the White House around the clock by opponents of EPI.

This morning, the protesters were visited by Senator Al Nathanson, a leading figure in the anti-EPI movement. "President Westwood likes to caricature these people as dangerous rabble-rousers, as threats to the security of this nation and this world of ours," the senator said. "But look around you. Open your eyes. Who do you see? Not terrorists. Not dangers to peace. You see mothers, fathers, children, decent people justly concerned at the possible consequences of the EPI and exercising their constitutional rights to express their views freely. And what, then, is the real threat? I'll tell you. It's miles above our heads, circling the Earth and armed with weaponry, the likes of which we've never seen before. The Guardian Star. I most strongly urge the president to reconsider this project while there is still time."

President Westwood himself, however, was in an uncompromising mood during a press conference held just a few hours ago. Describing the protesters as "misguided and mistaken," the president claimed that the

Guardian Star was "the future," and to oppose it was "like trying to take a stand against tomorrow."

"I question the motives of many of those who would see us defenseless," he went on to say. "The enemy is not to be found in space. The true enemy is among us now. We must be ever watchful . . ."

"I'm telling you," Eddie protested, "it wasn't my fault."

"We know that, Eddie," sighed Cally. "You've been telling us ever since we fished you out of the lake. But it *is* your shot, so why don't you take it and give us all a break."

"Give us a break?" Eddie examined the lie of the balls on the rec room's pool table. "You making a joke there, Cal?"

They were playing pairs. It was Eddie and Bex versus Cally and Jake, with Ben and Lori standing by to face the winners.

Eddie made a token attempt to line up a shot but then groaned in apparent pain. "Ow. I don't know, guys. I don't think I can get down that low."

"That'd be a first," grunted Jake.

"No, it's the old back. Think I pulled it narrowly cheating almost-certain death this morning. You know I nearly died today."

"Poor thing," soothed Bex. "What you need is the touch of a healing hand." She leaned her cue against the table. "And it just so happens I have two. How does this feel?" She began to massage Eddie's lower back.

"Ah, good, good. Better." Eddie's eyelids fluttered. "But lower. A bit lower, Bex. I can feel a run coming on."

"There?" Her fingers flexed downward until they found the belt of his jeans.

"Well, actually, Bex, any chance of lower still? I'm really starting to feel a whole lot better."

"No chance at all." She slapped his back, and Eddie yelped. "And you can heal yourself in the future, you fraud."

"Okay, okay." He leaned over the table and cracked the cue ball. His aim was perfect. "Just talk among yourselves while I clean up, will you? Won't be long." Ball after ball dropped docilely into the pockets.

"Well, whatever went wrong with Eddie's SkyBike we'll soon know," Lori said. "The technicians are supposed to be working on it now, aren't they?"

"Probably just a glitch," said Jake. "Pity something similar's not affecting his game."

Ben wasn't so frivolous. "We don't get 'probably just glitches' at Spy High," he observed. "There's got to be something more. And what about Lacey's cousin going mad and threatening those people, then blowing herself up? That doesn't make sense either."

Everyone had heard about the rampage of Mary Bannon on the news and had been suitably shocked. Their weapons instructor had apparently been given a few days off to attend her relative's funeral.

"What, you think the two things are connected, Ben?" Cally sounded skeptical.

Ben shrugged. "They're both linked to the school, aren't they? Mary Bannon tenuously, I know, but didn't we learn from Threat Analysis to look for connections?"

"You're getting paranoid, Benny boy," tutted Jake.

"Yeah. This cousin thing," said Bex. "I mean, families. Who can understand them?"

"You think?" The glare that Ben was directing at Jake converted into an expression of sly interest as he turned toward Bex.

"Are you speaking from personal experience, Rebecca? Sorry, I mean Bex. Only you don't talk much about your background, do you?"

"There's a lot of things I don't talk much about." Bex met Ben's eyes and smiled, he thought almost tauntingly. "But you're a secret agent, Ben, nearly at any rate. If you're so interested, figure out my background for yourself."

"Can we keep the confrontation down a bit?" Eddie implored from his position spread-eagled across the pool table. "I'm trying to sink the eightball here."

Ben wasn't listening. The others might as well not have been there, just him and Bex. There *was* something, a secret. He was sure of it, now more than ever. She was hiding something. She didn't deserve to be one of them. She wasn't good enough. "Give me a clue," he said. "Hometown? Everybody's got a hometown, don't they?"

Bex was aware that, with the exception of Eddie, her teammates were watching her, not suspiciously, not with hostility, but they seemed to be with Ben in expecting an answer. So she gave them one. "Hometown? Okay. Try Cadnam, Massachusetts."

Try it, indeed, thought Ben. He could have hugged himself. The Stantons had holdings in Cadnam, Massachusetts. "I know it well," he said. "So that means you must have gone to Anderson High before you got selected for Deveraux."

"That's right." Was he imagining it, or did Bex's smile seem fixed and artificial? Was he on to something here? "See? You don't need me to tell you anything."

"Guess not. Nice town, Cadnam." His own smile wasn't exactly genuine, either. "I used to play baseball in Grove Park when we visited. You might even have seen me, Bex, and not known it."

"I might have," said Bex.

You'd have had a job, Ben thought darkly. There was no such place. Bex was lying. She clearly knew *of* Cadnam, but she just as clearly wasn't *from* there. Curiouser and curiouser. But if he wanted to pursue the matter now, he didn't get the chance.

Eddie had sunk the eightball. With a shout of triumph worthy of the winning shot in a world championship, he threw his arms around Bex and danced a circle. "I thank you, I thank you, I thank you. The victors: Nelligan and Dee!"

"Stupid game, anyway," grumbled Jake.

"Looks like you're up," said Cally, handing her cue to Lori.

Only it wasn't to be. Senior Tutor Elmore Grant entered the rec room. He didn't look happy. "Don't tell me he bet on Jake and Cal," said Eddie. Maybe, because he headed straight for the Bond Team.

But maybe not. "I thought you ought to know," he said. "The technicians have completed their analysis of that faulty bike. Eddie was not in any way to blame for what happened."

"Told you."

"I'm afraid the machine had already been tampered with." Grant paused. "It looks very much like sabotage."

Strictly speaking, the students were not allowed to attempt the Gun Run without the supervision of a teacher. Something to do with health and safety regulations. Which itself seemed rather ironic to Ben, that health and safety regulations should be applied to an exercise whose purpose it was to do some damage. And for once, he was willing to bend the rules. Weapons

Instructor Lacey Bannon might still be on leave, but he wasn't prepared to wait for her return before giving himself a good, violent workout. Ben needed to get rid of some stress, and shooting animates on the Gun Run was just the ticket. There was a tech present to operate the program. That was health and safety enough.

"You're stressed, aren't you?" Lori observed. "What you need is a shoulder massage to unlock all that tension. If I didn't have a shock blaster in my hand . . ."

"Maybe later," said Ben. "Let's try staying alive first."

The two of them were standing in a bedroom. Ben had opted for the house program, about the simplest and most straightforward scenario the Gun Run could offer. The bedroom, and the rest of the house, too, if he and Lori wanted to explore it, seemed at the moment empty and normal, but as soon as the run was activated, animates — faceless and murderous mannequins — would appear from any and all directions, like they'd suddenly heard there was a party going on, and drinks were free. The students' task was to reach the front door and exit the house intact. Ben and Lori had managed it several times already. Now wasn't likely to be any different.

"Okay," Ben directed the technician via his shock suit's communicator, "let's see some action."

In response, a starter bell rang. It woke up the man who'd apparently been sleeping beneath the covers of the bed, the man with no face with an automatic weapon. He clearly hadn't wanted to be disturbed. His gun blazed. Ben and Lori dived left and right, both executing perfect forward rolls, aiming and firing at the same time with their shock blasters. The man slumped back down on the bed. Permanently.

Wooden applause from wardrobe doors as they slammed open. Killers in the closets. On one knee, Ben and Lori took them out, the animates pitching forward riddled with holes.

"Ben!" Lori's warning was sufficient. He saw movement under the bed. A good place to hide, maybe, but not a good place to shoot from. Ben ended the threat with a single squeeze of the trigger. "The room is cleared out, I think," Lori said. "Feeling better?"

"Starting to."

Lori got to her feet. "You shouldn't be worrying about the SkyBike business, Ben. You know that, don't you?"

"Do I?" Ben also stood up. He didn't like being looked down on. "It's just that 'sabotage' is the kind of word that's on my blacklist. You know, along with 'betrayal' and 'killed in the line of duty.'"

"But Grant thinks it wasn't sabotage with the intention of really hurting someone. You heard him, Ben. A prank that went wrong, that's what he said."

"Yeah? Well, with pranksters like that at Spy High, we'd all better start writing our wills. Besides," Ben narrowed his eyes, "that's not the only thing."

"No?"

"No."

An overeager animate from the landing burst into the bedroom. Lori gunned it down in irritation. "Don't you know it's rude to interrupt when people are talking?" She kicked its legs out of the way to enable her to shut the door again. Shock blasts crackled along the doorframe. She glimpsed dark figures moving menacingly toward them. "I think you'd better tell me what the 'not the only thing' is, Ben," she said. "The natives are getting restless."

"Okay." He had to share it with someone, and Lori was supposed to be his girlfriend. *Supposed to be, but what about Jake?* "It's Bex. She's hiding something."

"Oh, Ben." Lori seemed dismayed. "I thought we were going to give her a chance."

"I did," Ben claimed. "She blew it. She's lying about her background, Lo."

"What?" Maybe she hadn't heard right over the gunfire from the landing.

"My family's got a place in Cadnam, Massachusetts, like I said. And what *she* said means she's probably never been through it on a bus let alone lived there."

"All right." Lori believed Ben implicitly. "But I'm sure there has to be a perfectly logical explanation, a reason."

"Like what?" Ben snorted. "I'm telling you, Lo, you can't trust anyone these days, not even your own teammates."

"What are you talking about?" Lori sensed Ben's hurt. "You can trust me." If she was expecting an immediate agreement, she didn't get one. "Ben, have I done something wrong?"

"Depends whether putting your arm around Jake Daly in the Hall of Heroes qualifies as something wrong, I guess." Even as he said it, even as he saw the disappointment in Lori's eyes because he'd said it, Ben felt petty and pathetic. "I saw you," he added lamely.

Lori sighed. "This must be your day for jumping to dumb conclusions, boyfriend, but I suppose I'd better set you straight on this one, at least. Look me in the eyes." Ben did so. He saw himself reflected in the crystal blue, small and sheepish. "I like Jake as a friend. I was comforting him because of Jennifer, that's all. That's what friends do where I come from."

"Yeah. Lori. I should have . . ." Apology was not a natural Stanton characteristic.

"Jake equals friend. Ben equals more than a friend, though I sometimes wonder why." Lori shook her head in tolerant exasperation. "Maybe this has got something to do with it." She kissed him full on the lips, kissed him deeply.

It seemed to have the desired effect. "I'm sorry, Lo," said Ben.

"You should be," she grinned, "but you can make it up to me once we get out of here."

Ben smiled, too. "Then what are we waiting for?"

They charged out of the bedroom with shock blasters ready, Lori aiming right, Ben left. Their coordination was icy cool and razor sharp, honed by hours of practice. The animates were fast, but the Spy High students were faster still. Nearest targets first — it was ingrained on Ben's mind — and shoot at the torso, the easiest mark to hit. He'd learned his lesson well. The impact of his shock blasts sent the animates sprawling backward. Alongside him, Lori was equally deadly. They hurtled along the landing and didn't miss once. Lacey Bannon would have been proud.

At the stairs: "Ben, take the lead! I'll cover you!" Back-to-back. The ground floor swarming with animates, armed, dangerous, and heading their way. Two were on the stairs already. Ben clasped his blaster with both hands for extra accuracy, fired once, twice, and cleared the way.

Lori was busy behind him. Clearing a reckless attack from another bedroom. She took an enemy out. A second and a third.

Her marksmanship was impeccable. With an automated cry, the animates crashed through the handrail and plunged to the floor below.

Shock blasts ricocheted from the banister and stairs as Ben and Lori fought their way downward, but the animates were programmed with only limited tactical awareness. They worked individually, not as a team. That meant they could be picked off individually. Ben and Lori's blasters were like scythes in a field of wheat. They gained the ground floor. There was an animate holding out behind a sofa. Lori's shot went right through the back of it and still found its target. And soon the only sound was the students breathing hard.

"All done?" Ben said, searching for any final source of assault.

"Looks like," Lori lowered her shock blaster, relaxing a little.

"Okay. Good." Ben nodded his approval. "I make that time to hit the showers. Anyone know where I can hire the services of an expert back-scrubber?" He sauntered toward the front door, pressed the exit button.

"Well, now that you mention it," Lori began, but that was as far as she got.

The front door remained stubbornly locked.

"What's going on here?" grumbled Ben. He tried the exit button again. And again. "This whole place is going to . . ." *The SkyBike. Sabotage.* Suddenly, the showers seemed a long way off. "Lori . . ."

There was a twitching of android limbs on the floor behind them. If the animates were never truly alive in the first place, could they now be truly dead?

"Uh, Ben." Lori watched the animates sit up, turn their

featureless faces toward them. Without eyes, how could they seem to be glaring? "I think maybe we could use some technical assistance."

"Ahead of you, Lo." Ben was frowning. "Only my suit communicator's gone silent on me. Try yours."

The animates were standing now. They were looking down at their strong synthetic hands as if wondering how to occupy them.

"Ketner, come in." The technician's name. "Ketner, can you hear me?" Evidently not. "The animates are walking."

"Closing in is more like it." Ben found that his back was pressing against the door. "On us." Their arms were extended, reaching out, fingers groping, grasping for something to squeeze. "Sorry, guys. Members of Bond Team are off-limits to malfunctioning animates."

"I don't think they're listening, Ben." Lori saw that they were surrounded. "I think we'd better just shoot them."

"Fair enough, Lo."

A fusillade of shock blasts. The animates staggered. The animates stumbled. But they kept on coming.

"They're supposed to fall. A hit's supposed to disengage their motor circuits." Lori seemed outraged that the mannequins were cheating. She fired with renewed vigor.

"We need to cut their power entirely!" Ben shouted above the shock blasts.

"How?"

"Aim high!"

"At their heads?"

"At the ceiling!"

The control panel, a glittering metal plate inlaid into the

ceiling. It provided the power for the entire house, like a brain in a body. Kill the brain and kill the body.

Good plan. Ben raised his arm. He couldn't miss. It couldn't have been easier if the control panel had colored circles and a bull's-eye painted on it. He squeezed the trigger. Correction: *would* have squeezed the trigger, only the lunging animate that clawed at his arms seemed to have other ideas. Like a clumsy dancing partner, the synthetic man wrestled with Ben, seemed to want to work his fist into Ben's mouth, down Ben's throat, to stop his breath like a five-fingered cork. The weight of the animate bore Ben down. He could hardly believe it, but all of a sudden, it looked like he was going to die. And that would leave Lori at the mercy of . . .

Lori. One shot was all she needed. The control panel exploded in a shower of sparks. At once, the house was doused with darkness. Better yet, the animates collapsed into ungainly heaps, their physical functions truly terminated. Ben thrust his now lifeless assailant away in disgust.

"You all right?" Lori asked.

"Good question." In the limited light, Ben's fury only made his expression seem even darker. "Think I'm worrying needlessly now, Lo? Do you think this was another prank that went wrong? I'm telling you, there's a saboteur loose at Spy High, and I'm betting that Bex Dee's somehow involved."

CHAPTER FOUR

IGC DATA FILE: MEDIA WATCH MW 300T
CATEGORY: Commercial
PRODUCT: Changing Faces Physical Reconstruction Clinics.
TEXT: Are you happy with who you are? When you look into the mirror, do you like what you see? And the people around you, at work, in the street, do they seem prettier or more handsome than you? Younger? Fitter? Leading more fulfilled and exciting lives?

It doesn't have to be that way. Now there's Changing Faces.

Changing Faces is your complete physical reconstruction clinic. We do not offer nips and tucks and superficial plastic surgery. What we can give you at Changing Faces is a total life overhaul, allowing you for the first time to really be who you want to be. From the most advanced facial remolding treatments available, to the latest tissue replacement programs, to painless height readjustment therapies, bone and muscle enhancements, even pioneering repigmentation surgery – Changing Faces provides it all, and at very reasonable rates. Our more-senior clients can also indulge themselves with our Fountain of Youth program, guaranteed to last to the grave.

So don't put up with the body God gave you. What did God know about physical reconstruction techniques, anyway? Resurrect your own life. Take your future into your own hands. Be who you want to be.

There's a Changing Faces clinic near you. Call toll-free. Call now.

Changing Faces Physical Reconstruction Clinics. Be who you want to be.

"A power surge?" Jake said skeptically.

All of Bond Team was gathered in the boys' room, sitting on

the beds and the chairs, with one notable exception: Bex was missing. It wasn't an oversight.

"That's what the tech said," Ben reiterated, "and that's what it'll apparently say on Grant's report to Deveraux. The Gun Run malfunctioned — and nearly killed Lori and me along the way, I might add — because of a freak power surge that overrode the safety protocols."

"But I didn't think that could happen." Cally frowned. "The system's designed to reroute any excess power back into the core."

"Yeah, but does the system know that?" Jake continued to doubt. "Me, I think systems suck."

"Ben won't tell you," said Lori, "but we also got reprimanded for engaging the Gun Run without Lacey being there. We've got to apologize to her when she comes back. So it hasn't been what you'd call a good day."

"Thanks for letting everybody know about that, Lo," scowled Ben. "Maybe you can take out an ad in the paper, as well. But I suppose it sums up the way things are going this term, doesn't it? There's a lunatic on the loose at Spy High trying to kill us, and it's us who end up getting in trouble. Makes perfect sense."

"I know what you're saying, Ben," Cally cautioned, "but statistically, two near fatal accidents still don't add up to one lunatic on the loose."

"And it doesn't mean that Bex has anything to do with it." Eddie, speaking for the first time, had rather more impact than the more usual scenario of Eddie speaking all the time. His teammates paused and looked at him. "I mean, that's why she's not here, isn't it? Why we're sneaking around, the Bond Team originals, holding secret meetings without her. *Isn't it?* Because Ben, for no apparent reason other than green hair and a few studs and apparently a tattoo somewhere, thinks she's a mole or a double agent or a dangerous subversive, like a punk rocker or something, which is probably even worse. Am I right?"

"Stick to making jokes, Eddie," said Ben coldly. "You're crappy at reasoned arguments. You're only sticking up for Bex because you like her."

"That's below the belt, Ben," winced Cally.

"I wish," said Eddie. "And you're only accusing her because you don't like her. I mean, where's your evidence?"

Ben told them about Cadnam, Massachusetts.

"Okay." Eddie considered. "Maybe she misheard you or something. It must be easy to mishear you when you've got half the Golden Gate Bridge in your ears. Maybe she thought you said Camden or Nandam or —"

"Don't bother, Eddie." Ben cut him short.

"Now I've got nothing against Bex," said Lori. "I quite like her. But we can't ignore what Ben's said. And it's maybe too much of a coincidence that virtually as soon as she arrives, Sky-Bikes and Gun Runs start spinning out of control."

"Power surge," muttered Eddie. "Happens all the time."

"I think we should go to Grant," Ben announced. "Report our suspicions."

"Maybe you're right, Ben," mused Cally. "I need to be able to trust who I'm working with."

Jake was pressing his lips together thoughtfully. "What about you, Lo? About Grant?"

"I don't think so." Lori didn't look at Ben. "At least, not yet. I think if we reported Bex and there was nothing in it, we'd never be able to function as a team again. How would she be able to forgive us?" She heard Ben snorting. "I think we should keep a subtle eye on her, watch her, just for a while. I think we can afford to wait."

"Let's vote on it," pressed Ben. *One minute she's all over me, the next she's opposing me.* What sort of girlfriend is she? "Those in favor of going to Grant?" Himself and Cally. Lori's hand remained resolutely in her lap. "Those in favor of waiting until Bex cuts our throats while we're sleeping?"

"Ben," objected Lori, pained.

"Sorry. Rephrase. Those in favor of waiting, period."

Eddie, of course, with both hands raised. And Lori, reluctantly but firmly. And finally, following her lead, Jake. Lori and Jake. Voting against him.

Ben might have said something he could well have regretted then but was saved, not by the bell, but by a confident, strident knock, immediately followed by the opening of the door.

Bex entered the room. She was smiling but her eyes fluttered between her teammates as if trying to read their minds. "Thought you might be here. Is this a private party or can anyone join in?"

"Bex," Ben said, with a bad attempt at friendliness, "we looked for you but couldn't find you."

"No," Bex laughed. "That rec room's elusive, isn't it?" Nobody was daring to catch her eye, not even Eddie. "Well, I'm here now." She closed the door behind her. "And then there were six."

"So what's going on between you and Ben?" Cally asked Lori the next day as they sipped Cokes in the rec room between lessons in Ethics in Espionage and Disabling Your Enemy: The Silent Kill.

"What do you mean? You know what's going on between me and Ben." Lori seemed uncomfortable. "Begins with *L* and rhymes with dove."

"Yeah? Still?" Cally probed. "Only lately I've been sensing there might be trouble in paradise." Lori flushed faintly. "Course, tell me to mind my own business if you want to, Lori. I've always been begins with *N* and rhymes with dozy."

"No, no," said Lori. "If you can't talk your problems through with a friend, who can you talk them through with?"

"So there is a problem? You and Ben?"

"No. Yes. I don't know." Lori shrugged helplessly. "All of the above, I guess. I still love Ben, Cal. I do. And he loves me, I'm sure of that. When we're together, it's . . . well, it's what you want it to be like when you're dreaming of boys. But I just wish Ben would take me more seriously at times."

"The blue-eyed-blond syndrome, huh?" Cally stroked her dreadlocks. "Not something I've ever had to worry about."

"Not quite," Lori pursued. "I mean, he respects my abilities as a spy, I know he does. We're equals on the team. But he doesn't really like me having my own opinions, expects me to support him and agree with him on everything — like with Bex. I think Ben thinks that's how girlfriends should behave. I kind of like to be independent."

"Too right," applauded Cally.

"So sooner or later, one of us is going to have to give in."

"And Ben doesn't like giving in, does he?" Cally leaned closer. "Lori, change the subject if you want, but do you ever wonder if maybe you started dating Ben too early, too soon. I mean, before you got to know him or any of the other boys here well enough to make, I don't know, the right choice?"

"Cally," said Lori, "I *am* going to change the subject. Look. Incoming."

It was Lacey Bannon. The weapons instructor, a woman responsible for many a hot flash and weak knee among the male population of the Spy High student body, normally entered rooms with a flourish, like a gunfighter into a saloon. This morning, though, accompanied by Mr. Korita from the martial arts department, she sidled in quietly, almost secretively, like a maiden aunt at a funeral. Of course. That was it.

"She must have just got back," said Cally. "Doesn't look good, does she?"

"Funeral duty isn't exactly R and R, Cal," Lori remarked, "particularly not when you think about how Lacey's cousin died."

They watched their tutors order coffee and settle at a table close by.

"You think we ought to go over and say hi or something?"

"Maybe," mused Lori. At some point, she knew, she and Ben were going to have to apologize to Lacey Bannon for what had happened on the Gun Run. She doubted that now was the appropriate moment. "Maybe we'd be intruding."

"Soon find out," said Cally. She squinted across to where Lacey was engaged in hushed conversation with her colleague. "I knew the old lip-reading lessons would come in handy sooner or later."

"Cally, you can't!" Lori was outraged but intrigued at the same time. They were training to be spies, after all. It was their job to find things out. And what had happened to Mary Bannon was so incredible. "All right, you can. What's she saying?"

"Little cousin Mary," reported Cally. "That's what they used to call her when they were children. 'Little Mary, meek and mild. She won't wed or have a child.' Excellent. That's gonna boost her self-esteem."

"Children can be cruel," observed Lori.

"Yeah, right," said Cally. "Can't we all? Lacey's worrying that what she and her brothers — I didn't know she had brothers — used to say about Mary might have affected her somehow, might be to blame for her going mad."

"She can't blame herself."

"That's what Mr. Korita's saying, and Lacey's kind of agreeing now. Apparently, Mary had been more confident lately, taken control of her life. She'd been to one of those — hold on . . ." Cally leaned forward, craned her neck.

"Cally!" Lori slapped her friend's shoulder. "Why not just go and ask them to speak up? They'll see you!"

"Don't fret. I'm in charge of the situation. Ah, and they're the words I'm looking for. Reconstruction clinics. She had some work done at one of those physical reconstruction clinics. Face. Body. You know. Or maybe you don't, Lo. Don't think you'll ever need to grace one with your looks."

"Cally, honestly. Give me a break."

"But Mary did. At somewhere called Changing Faces. She was going to be a new woman. Apparently, that was the last thing she and Lacey talked about."

"Really?" Lori seized Cally's arm and tugged. "And it's certainly the last thing we're going to be eavesdropping on. Lip-reading tutors is probably an expellable offense. Come on. Let's go."

"Whatever you say, Lo." Cally grinned. "You're probably right. We wouldn't want to get expelled, would we?"

IGC DATA FILE GRT 3307

. . . at least a hundred people leaping to their deaths from the Hovertel Hilton claiming that the place was ablaze and about to explode. No trace of fire was found.

This tragic and bizarre affair is the latest in what is becoming an increasingly long and worrying list of fatal incidents involving apparently sane individuals suddenly behaving in quite irrational and often homicidal ways. These include the Mary Bannon incident and the Nelson Nolan submersibubble disaster. In a bid to explain the trend, experts are beginning to talk about a new form of mental illness which they have termed "futurephobia."

Professor of psychology at George W. Bush University, Reiner Eichstein, puts it thus: "We live in an age of great, unparalleled social and scientific change. New ideas and novel ways of life are becoming available all the time. The certainties of yesterday seem a long way away, the technologies of today seem scarcely comprehensible, and as for the prospect of tomorrow, well, to increasing numbers of people the world, the future seems more like a threat than a promise, a world, which they fear they will not be able to understand and in which they worry they will have no place. In extreme cases, this dread of the future can create and is creating a clinical phobia in the minds of citizens, a phobia that without treatment may find expression in sudden, unpredictable outbursts of violence and rage . . ."

It wouldn't have been fair to say that Bex moving about in the room actually woke her up — Lori had only managed an unsatisfactory doze so far, her mind restless with thoughts of Ben, Lacey Bannon and even, from somewhere, Jake — but it *did* prevent her from going back to sleep. Particularly as Bex seemed, for some reason, to have put her clothes on. And particularly as she seemed to be heading, not for the bathroom, as might have been expected at two in the morning, but for the door to the corridor, glancing behind her surreptitiously in order to check that her roommates remained slumbering.

She ought to have checked more closely.

As Bex slipped out of the door, Lori slipped out of bed and into her sneakers. Where could Bex be stealing to at this time of night? Ben's warning whispered in her head: *"I'm telling you, there's a saboteur loose in Spy High, and I'm betting that Bex Dee's somehow involved."* What if he was right? On both counts? And after she'd stood against him. Lori peeked at a sweetly snoozing Cally. Better not to wake her, too. Silent pursuit was simpler when done solo.

She eased herself out into the corridor, swapping looks left and right as if about to cross a busy road. Bex to the right, and turning right, too, in the night-light seemed like a ghost, like a shadow. Lori followed her, gliding swiftly and as noiselessly as her battered old sneakers would allow. It occurred to her that maybe she should have paused to throw a robe over her nightie, but then it also occurred to her that had she done that, she'd have probably lost sight of Bex entirely. If she encountered somebody else, she could always plead somnambulism.

It was lucky the corridors at Spy High were long. Lori gained the right turn in time to see Bex take the stairs. But not down, to the common room, the rec room, the library, or the studies, but up, to the floor above. Where the private areas belonging to the tutors were: Lacey, Grant, Mr. Korita, even access to the holiest of holies, Jonathan Deveraux's suite itself. Why was she heading there? Perplexed and intrigued, Lori hurried to the stairs.

A darker shadow than the rest was lurching about above her. Lori judged that it was swinging to the left. When it had disappeared so that she could safely scale the stairs, left was the direction she'd need to take at the top.

It was a dead end. Past Mr. Korita's rooms, past Grant's, past the always-sealed door to Jonathan Deveraux's accommodation, which, while accessed from here, did in fact occupy the entire top floor of the school. Lori passed them all. And reached the window in the far wall — the window that was closed from the inside. Even if Bex had wanted to vacate the premises by this inexplicable and unlikely route, she'd have had to have melted through solid brick and glass to do it, a skill not even Spy High taught. She couldn't have come this way after all. Yet Lori was still certain that she had.

So much for her A-plus in the Stealth Techniques class. Paper qualifications, as Eddie "C minus" Nelligan always said. Not worth the ink they're written in when it comes to the real world.

Lori suddenly felt very foolish. What if Grant or somebody should come out of their room and find her here? How could she explain herself? She was in enough trouble already after the Gun Run.

Time for bed. And maybe a pointed word with Bex in the morning.

Though she didn't need to wait that long, not if she didn't want to. When Lori returned to their room, Bex was already there, and sleeping soundly as if she hadn't stirred for hours.

Some schools might have been able to match Spy High's sporting and recreational facilities, others might have boasted of superior classroom accommodation, or a more extensive library, but no other school in the country, if not the world, could equal the virtual reality chamber. Most governments didn't even have access to such advanced virtual technology. The oval room, lined with the gleaming steel and glass capsules of the cyber-cradles, stood as testimony to the genius of Deveraux Academy's former inventor-in-chief, Professor Henry "Gadge" Newbolt. Sadly for Gadge, time had gradually turned his brain to putty, reducing him to an imaginary world of his own, wandering the corridors of Spy High in a white coat and toying with circuits and wires in his lab like a child playing with bricks. But for the students at the school, he had provided a most stimulating legacy.

"This your first time, Bex?" probed Eddie. "I mean, me, I've done it loads of times. It really helps if you just relax and enjoy yourself. Here, let me —"

Bex slapped the boy's overeager hands away. "Eddie, I appreciate the offer but I have been in a cyber-cradle before."

"At your previous school, of course," Ben chipped in from the cradle to the other side of Bex. He was already seated inside and about to lie down.

"Of course."

"Then you know what to expect, don't you? The unexpected." Ben smiled like there was some kind of subtext in what he'd just said. "You can never tell what's real and what's not."

"Thanks for the advice, Mr. Cryptic," said Bex. "I'll keep it in mind."

"Less talk, more action," berated Corporal Keene, in charge of the session. "Dee, Nelligan, we haven't got all day." He paced briskly up and down as if trying to keep warm.

Lori watched Eddie and Bex climb into their respective cyber-cradles. She'd been keeping a furtive eye on Bex all day as it happened, though without daring to confront her over her late night walkabout. She hadn't told Ben, either. In the cold light of day, it actually seemed more like something she'd dreamed rather than witnessed firsthand.

"Angel, have you suddenly developed a back problem?" snapped Corporal Keene.

"No, sir."

"Then I suggest you lie on it. I'm activating the transfer program now."

Lori dutifully stretched out on the leather quilting of the cyber-cradle, crossing her hands on her chest like she was about to ascend to heaven. She reminded herself of the stone effigies of medieval ladies that had often been carved on the tops of their tombs. It was as well she didn't suffer from claustrophobia. The virtual sensors pressed gently, almost lovingly, against her temples. With a motherly sigh, the cradle's glass shield lowered and clicked into place, shutting her in. Lori felt the warm hum of the transference into the virtual world. She felt her mind being lifted out of her body, her sight grow dim. She closed her eyes and let herself drift.

"Another location that's hardly in the running for this year's top-ten holiday destinations," Eddie was already moaning.

Lori opened her eyes. She and the rest of the Bond Team were in the rusting metal corridor of what seemed to be some kind of factory complex. Intermittent light, like the final gasps of a dying man. Grime, oil, and decay, the stench of despair and decomposition.

"You want sun, sand, and surf, Ed," advised Cally with a grin, "then you'd better flunk school and go join the tourist board."

"And leave you all to go on without me, Cal?" Eddie grinned back. "That just wouldn't be fair."

Jake sniffed, furrowed his brow. "Does the air in here seem bad to you guys?"

"This is an abandoned nuclear power facility," Ben reminded them, "somewhere in Siberia. The Russians weren't big on air fresheners, Jake. The scenario is that a rogue terrorist group has seized control —"

"I know what the scenario is, Ben," Jake interrupted tetchily. "The briefing was in English. I'm just finding it a bit heavy on the lungs in here, that's all."

"Are they always like this?" Bex was suddenly at Lori's shoulder. "Ben and Jake, I mean. Displays of testosterone are so tedious, aren't they?"

Lori resented the implied criticism of the two boys. "They can work together when they need to," she said, and here was her chance. "By the way, Bex, I've been meaning to ask. Did you sleep well last night?"

For a second, a glimpse of surprise, even panic, in Bex's eyes, quickly mastered. "I always sleep well. It comes from having a clear conscience."

Lori might have said something to that, but Cally's coughing stopped her. Cally doing more than coughing. Cally gasping, choking, clutching at her throat. "Cal? Cally?" Everyone gathering around her. "What's wrong?"

"Can't . . . breathe . . ."

And then Eddie suddenly gasping, too, his mouth wide and straining.

"Is this in the scenario?" Jake turned to Ben.

"No." Emphatically. "Something's . . ." *The SkyBike. The Gun Run. Three strikes and you're out.* Ben paled almost physically. "The saboteur . . ." And he couldn't breathe. There was a pressure on his chest and he couldn't breathe. Jake, Lori, all of them were struggling now, as if the air itself had been sucked out of the program. Eddie and Cally were on their knees, floundering, suffocating.

They were suffocating. All of them.

Except Bex.

Even as Ben felt his legs buckling beneath him, he could see that Bex was unaffected. She seemed truly horrified, watching her teammates die, but whatever it was that was afflicting the five of them, Bex appeared immune.

Ben pointed an accusing finger. "You . . ." he croaked. It was all he had time for.

CHAPTER FIVE

Somehow, Cally was on the floor, slumped against rusted pipes with pools of dank water staining the trousers of her shock suit. Her throat was hurting and it was like she'd forgotten how to breathe. She needed to remember again pretty soon.

Her vision seemed to be blurring but was that Bex leaning over her? "What's happening? Cally, can you hear me?" Was she saying that? How come Bex could breathe?

And then, was that Keene looming, too, entering the virtual world himself as instructors had the right to do? "End program immediately!" Was he really that agitated? "Initiate transfer sequence now!"

"I didn't do anything!" Bex seemed to be crying. "I didn't do anything!"

Cally felt herself slipping away, falling into an ocean of impossible colors that crashed at her senses in scintillating waves. Cyberspace. Her mind was between realities and everything was cool. Everything was all right. She felt like she could stay here forever.

Only she couldn't. Not if she wanted to live.

Think of what happened before, think of how you were trapped in your cyber-sleep and nearly died. Think of Nemesis, what it tried to do to you.

She had to get out.

Cally's consciousness lurched into the cyber-cradle. The sensors clung to her temples like sticky fingers. The cradle's glass shield refused to rise. And she still could not breathe. Cyber-cradle. Cyber-coffin. She thumped feeble fists against the glass, pounded like the beating of a heart about to burst.

She'd have screamed but she had no air. Somehow, the air had been pumped out.

In the chamber beyond her, technicians shouted and scurried. The systems must have failed. They were trying to open her cyber-cradle manually, maybe the others, too. It wasn't working. Cally felt her stomach squeezing. If they didn't manage it soon, they needn't bother at all.

And then Keene again, looming again, yelling once more. And this time he was armed with a pulse rifle. He was aiming it directly at her. Would a hole in her stomach let the air in? He was pulling the trigger.

The glass shield of Cally's cyber-cradle, reinforced and specially treated, did not shatter with the first blast, but it did shake. A million cracks, like a spider's web patterned her prison. But she couldn't smash her way out. No strength. Her hands were at her throat as her back bucked. One last chance to survive. Only one.

Keene fired again. This time Cally did find a strangled scream as shards of glass showered her writhing form. The second pulse had punched its way through. Some of the splinters nicked her face, her hands, lodged in her dreadlocked hair like cheap jewelry, but a few scratches were a small price to pay for continued breath.

"Sit forward, Cally." Technician hands helped her. "Breathe slowly, deeply. That's it. You're all right now."

She thought she might be, though her limbs were trembling and weak. Keene had left her cyber-cradle and was assaulting the next in line. Two other technicians with pulse rifles were doing likewise. One by one, her teammates were released gulpingly, gaspingly into the safety of the virtual reality chamber.

Out of the corner of her eye, Cally saw Senior Tutor Elmore Grant observing the operation. Her body language studies — good for assessing whether the young man you were about to turn your back on was indeed as charming as he looked or a dangerously psychotic foreign agent about to slip a knife between your ribs — told her that he was standing in a defensive posture, legs planted wide apart, arms crossed, chin thrust resolutely forward. He looked like a senior tutor with a lot on his mind. Like the near suffocation of an entire team of spies in training. Or actually, the near suffocation of a near-entire team.

Bex was hovering nervously at Grant's side, biting on bright green fingernails. Bex hadn't needed the assistance of a pulse rifle to exit her cyber-cradle. Cally wondered why. It was a question that also seemed to be concerning the rest of her teammates.

They gathered together instinctively as the techs helped them from the cradles. Cally tottered a little, but Jake was there to hold her arm, his fingers still surprisingly strong. Lori and Ben were supporting each other. Only Eddie seemed to be swaying like he'd been pilfering from the liquor cabinet and was in need of a prop. Bex looked like she was approaching him to provide precisely that service.

Only Ben stepped in her way. "Where d'you think you're going?"

"To see if you're all okay, of course," Bex said guardedly. "Is that a problem?"

Ben chuckled grimly. "Is that a problem, she says. Did you hear her, Lo?"

"Ben . . ." Lori cautioned, but halfheartedly.

"I'll tell you what the real problem is, Bex, Rebecca, or whatever you're actually called —" Ben was accelerating toward full-on rant mode —"the real problem is why you're the only one of us whose cyber-cradle didn't turn psycho and try to strangle you. What have you got that the rest of us haven't, huh?"

"I don't know what you mean, Ben."

"Coincidence, Bex. I don't believe in it. Whatever happens, happens for a reason."

Bex turned to the others, tried to laugh. It sounded hollow. "Think our noble leader's in need of medical attention, guys, don't you? Lack of oxygen can cause brain damage, you know that? And if your brain's small in the first place —"

"I think you'd better stop there, Bex," said Lori stonily.

Bex did. Her teammates' faces were closed against her. Only Eddie did not appear directly hostile, but even he couldn't catch her eye. "All right," dared Bex. "If you want to make accusations, don't leave 'em at a hint. Come right out with them. Let's see what you've got."

"Nobody's accusing anyone of anything," intervened Corporal Keene rather optimistically. "Why don't we all just calm down?"

"I'm sorry, sir," Ben protested, "but that's where you're wrong. I mean, what was this? Another power surge? There's a saboteur in our midst and if nothing's done soon, someone's gonna die. And I *am* accusing Bex, of not being who she says she is."

"What are you talking about, Stanton?" Keene seemed puzzled.

"She lied about her background. I know she did. Ask her."

"That's crazy, ridiculous." Even so, Bex found herself taking a step back. "Ben's obviously delusional, can't you see that?"

Evidently, the rest of Bond Team couldn't see that. For once, Jake was shoulder-to-shoulder with Ben. "Can't we maybe vote for a new leader? I mean, why would I lie?"

"That's what we'd like to know," said Cally.

"Whatever happened in virtual reality, whatever happened to the cradles —" Bex was starting to lose her cool —"it has nothing to do with me. I don't understand it any more than you do. I mean, why would I . . ." In frustration she sought reinforcements. "Mr. Grant . . ."

"All right, Bex, that will do." Grant stepped forward. His face was like a mask, impossible to read. "This little confrontation has gone on long enough. If you'd like to leave, I need a brief word with your teammates." Bex hesitant. Bond Team baffled. "If you'd like to leave," Grant repeated, gently but insistently. Bex left.

Ben watched her depart with the pained expression of a cop forced to look on as a burglar made good on his escape. "But, sir, what about —?"

Grant raised his hand for silence. "You need to listen, Ben, not ask questions. All of you do. It seems I have an apology to make. Evidently I underestimated the significance of those previous incidents with the SkyBike and the Gun Run, but not anymore. Like Ben, I have difficulties with coincidence. Today was nearly a disaster, and clearly not an accidental one. The integrity of Spy High's computer systems has obviously been compromised."

"But how, sir?" Lori asked. "And by who?"

"Somebody highly dangerous, that's certain," said Grant unnecessarily, "and until we apprehend him — or her — I'm increasing our security status to code red. All computer-controlled training and recreational facilities are also out of action until further notice."

"Any chance of suspending lessons entirely?" hoped Eddie.

"Not one," said Grant. "But be careful, all of you. Coincidence, again: All three incidents have involved Bond Team. No one else."

"You think this is personal, sir?" Jake's eyes narrowed.

"I think you need to be alert, as your training has taught you."

"But sir, about Bex." Ben was nothing if not persistent. "What I was saying —"

"Is irrelevant, Ben," dismissed Grant. "It's the final thing I need to tell you before I want you to go to the infirmary for a checkup. Bex is not involved with any of this. That much I can guarantee. You can trust her."

"Sir? But she's lied to us." Ben wasn't convinced.

"There's no argument about this, Ben," Grant stressed. "Whoever our saboteur is, it isn't Bex. And that's the end of the matter."

Ben looked like he was about to suggest that he didn't think so, but Lori tugged his sleeve and kept him quiet.

"Now if there's nothing else," Grant concluded, "the infirmary, and excused classes for the rest of the day. Keene, a word, please." The two teachers left the chamber.

"Excused classes?" Eddie said gleefully. "Maybe we should get half-suffocated more often."

Ben wasn't amused. "What does he know about Bex that we don't? There's something, that's for sure."

The others seemed to agree, though Eddie only reluctantly. "So what do we do?" Lori wanted to know.

Ben's eyes were chips of blue ice. "I'm not waiting for another attack like today." He regarded his teammates conspiratorially. "I think it's time we took charge of our own security."

"Bex! Hey, Bex! Wait up!"

She didn't. Whether she might have slowed down had the pursuing voice belonged to anyone but Eddie, it was impossible to tell. But if anything, Bex increased her pace as she headed out of the school building and toward the athletics track. "Not now, Eddie, I'm going for a run."

"Yes, now." Eddie jogged to catch up with her, overtake her, block her path. "And there's no running away from this. Or me."

"Okay, okay." Bex shrugged her submission. "So what do you want?"

"To help."

"Say again? To help?" Bex sounded scornful. "What makes you think I need any help, Eddie? Do I look like an invalid to you?"

"I'm on your side, Bex."

"I thought we were all supposed to be on the same side." With bitterness. "It says Bond *Team* on the door, am I right? Not Bond Group of Suspicious and Distrustful Individuals."

"I know," Eddie agreed, "but the others . . ." He groped for words like a blind man in an unfamiliar room. One-liners weren't any use in a situation like this, and Eddie's serious-talk-with-girls vocabulary was still at primer stage. "You've got to try and see things from their point of view, Bex. I mean, you're new, a stranger. According to Ben you've told us some lies about your past . . ."

"I thought you were supposed to be on my side, Eddie."

"I am. I really want to be. I mean, I like you, Bex." Uncomfortably, almost embarrassedly. "I really like you . . ."

"That's nice, partner. I feel a whole lot better. Can I go now?"

"Listen, I'm trying to be serious here." Eddie's eyes flashed indignantly. "I could be about the only ally you've got, and I want to know something or you could end up entirely on your own. What Ben said — Cadnam, Massachusetts. Is it true?"

Bex regarded Eddie with a new interest, almost with respect. She seemed to reach a decision within herself. "All right," she said. "It's true. I lied."

Eddie groaned. "But why? I mean, Bex, how can you expect us to trust you?"

"The same way you'd trust anyone else, Eddie." Earnestly. "Faith. Belief. You've got to have faith in me, regardless of appearances. Things aren't always what they seem."

"So tell me what they are. Tell the others."

"I can't." Bex shook her head. "I can't. All I can tell you, Eddie, and I'm telling you because you're the only one who's actually come after me and asked me for my side of the story, is that I'm a friend, not an enemy. My reasons for taking a few liberties with my past are not what Ben thinks." Eddie opened his mouth to speak again, but Bex silenced him with a finger on his lips. "I can't tell you what they are. Don't ask, Eddie. You're just going to have to have that little bit of faith and keep trusting me. Stay on my side, Eddie. Please."

"Sure." Bex's gaze was turning his knees to jelly. She was really close to him now. "You can rely on me, Bex."

"I knew that already. Thanks." She kissed him, briefly and

not on the lips, but Eddie didn't care about that. You always get an appetizer before the main course. "Now I'd better go do my run before my tracksuit wonders why I put it on. See you."

"Guaranteed," said Eddie. He watched Bex lope toward the track. Trust her? Absolutely. Though part of him did wonder if he'd be quite as willing to do so if he didn't also fancy her like mad.

A room with no windows. A room with no chair.

The girl is standing. She is strong on her legs. Her body beneath the single clinging garment she wears is lithe and supple. As ever, she stares ahead, into space, into thought, and her eyes are cold and her lips are pressed tight.

She is not alone. There are six others with her in the room with no windows. Five of them encircle her, three male, two female. Their features are familiar. Two of them are blond. One of them is dark. One of them has red hair. One of them is black. A man, the man who has been here before, stands outside the circle and observes. Hands with long fingers rub together. They twine like worms. There is eagerness in his eyes.

"Begin," he says.

The girl is a blur of motion. She bludgeons the blond female before she can even mount a defense. She leaps into the air, whirling with deadly limbs. A kick and the redhead is senseless. Lethal fists beat the blond boy to the floor. Not once does she pause. Her actions are those of an automaton, a fighting machine. Her flesh is like steel. Her form is a weapon. The black girl attacks but she is blocked, effortlessly, instinctively, and then a ruthless rain of blows beats her down. Not once does the girl make a sound. Her opponents try to rise, but she does not permit it. They fall beneath her and lie still on the floor of the room with no windows.

Only one assailant remains. The dark-haired male. He kicks but she evades his attack, drops low, bunching her muscles. She springs. She strikes. Dark Hair struggles, cries out as she locks her arms around his fragile neck and twists. Savagely. Without thought. In the room with no windows, there is nobody left for the girl to fight.

She allows herself a cry of victory. It is cold and cruel, inhuman, and if heard at night would curdle the blood. The silence was better.

Or even the applause of the onlooking man. "Oh, well done, my dear. Well done, indeed." Like the director of a play, the man who pulls the strings. "Your finest performance yet. And how do you feel? How did that make you feel, hmm?"

"Feel?" She's scarcely breathing faster. She looks down at those she has defeated. The idea of feeling seems alien to her. "I feel nothing. I feel good."

"Excellent," approves the man. "You've made me so proud of you, my dear, my child, I believe it to be time for the treat I promised you." He presses a control on his wrist. In the wall of the room with no windows, a door appears. It opens noiselessly and there is blackness beyond. "You are ready at last, my dear. It is time to take my plans toward completion, toward our mutual fulfillment." He bows and gestures gallantly. "After you, my dear."

"You are keeping an eye out, Jake, right?"

"Two eyes and twenty-twenty vision, leader man. Good enough for you?"

"Excellent. Even better without the sarcasm."

Ben was nervous, understandably so. The last time they'd had Cally hack into Spy High's confidential and for-staff-eyes-only personal records, when they'd been trying to locate Jennifer's possible whereabouts, Ben had been against it. Breaking the rules just didn't sit easily with him. And even now, desperate as he was to discover the truth about Bex, he was still worried about the consequences of being found here in the computer suite at two in the morning. But what choice did they have? So Jake was guarding the door while Ben, Lori, and an unusually quiet Eddie watched Cally perform her keyboard magic.

"No need to panic, Ben," she assured him. "I'm nearly there. Bypassing a security program is like riding a SkyBike. You've done it once, you never forget how."

"And you didn't disturb Bex on your way out?" Ben asked.

"Sleeping like a baby." Lori's turn for reassurance. "And even if she woke up now, why would she ever imagine we'd be here?"

"Right," muttered Eddie. "Why would she think her supposed teammates are dong a number on her?"

"Something on your mind, Eddie?" Ben said. "Or should I be aiming a little lower?"

"You can get low, Ben. No doubt about that."

"No bickering," Cally snapped. "You might want to look this way." The computer screen now bore Bex's name and an invitation to enter her file. "No need to applaud, but I thank you, anyway. I assume we want in?"

"You're very talented," said Ben, "and you assume right."

"Okay," Cally grinned. "Here goes. Hold on to your prejudices."

She clicked on ENTER.

The lights went out. The computer crashed.

"What? What's going on?" All of Bond Team were shadows in darkness. Cally stood, clutched for the others. "I've got a bad feeling about this," somebody moaned.

"Let's go," Ben urged. "Back to our rooms. If the power's failed, there'll be security about. We mustn't be found here." He was already in enough trouble with Grant.

"Hey, there's somebody . . ." Jake's voice from the void where the door used to be. "Wait! Who . . . ?" And then a punching sound, a groan, and the thud of a body falling and striking the floor.

"Jake!" cried Lori, darting into darkness.

"Lori!" Ben pursued.

"I knew I should have stayed in bed," sighed Eddie. "Cally, shall we?"

They found Jake by almost tripping over him. He was stunned but seemed otherwise unhurt. "Someone get the number of that truck."

"What happened, Jake?" Lori was kneeling by him. She was probably stroking his brow. Ben didn't need to physically see it to recognize its likelihood.

"I saw . . . somebody . . . moving in the darkness. Somebody with a good right hook."

"We'll worry about that later." Ben wished that Jake would just get up. "We've got to move before —"

Before the lights went on again, as suddenly as they were extinguished. Before they found themselves confronted by Corporal Keene and several of the school's security personnel. Before it was too late.

"Well, well," said Corporal Keene, "and what have we here?"

* * *

A nightmare, Ben thought gloomily. It was all turning into a nightmare, and somehow he sensed that the worst was still to come.

They were marched to Grant's study where, giving no impression that he'd just been roused from his bed, if the senior tutor had been a weather system, he'd have been a tropical storm about to become a hurricane. He glowered at Bond Team in a manner that made Cally, for one, shudder. She'd never seen Grant look at anyone that way before. Without sympathy. Without understanding. Without mercy. It occurred to Cally that events were quickly slipping out of their control.

"We can explain, sir." Ben's opening gambit.

"Really, Stanton?" Stanton, not Ben, and an iciness in the tone that suggested any explanation had better be good. Lori thought she saw faint surprise register even on the normally implacable face of Corporal Keene.

"The reason we were in the computer suite," Ben stumbled on. "It was all my idea. The others, they aren't to blame —"

"I don't care why you were in the computer suite," announced Grant.

"You don't?" Ben was baffled.

"I care why you were in the central control room earlier today."

"What?" Bafflement became dawning fear. A *nightmare,* Ben reminded himself. He saw his own anxiety reflected in the expressions of the others. "But we haven't been in the central control room, sir, not earlier, not ever."

"Ah, but the camera says you have, Stanton," Grant gloated. "The hidden camera, the one you evidently didn't notice." He raised his voice. "Desk. Playback."

The flat surface of Grant's smart-desk flickered and became a videoscreen. It showed the interior of what Bond Team took to be the central control room, all lights and circuits and computers. But it wasn't the interior decoration of the central control room that caught their attention, made them breathe sharply inward, almost in unison. It was the presence of five instantly recognizable but at the same time utterly impossible figures in the room, each engaged in serial tampering with the equipment. Themselves.

"So," observed Grant coldly, "I think we know now who our saboteurs are."

"No." Ben could scarcely manage even that. His jaw seemed locked.

"And why you sought to discredit Dee, because she wasn't in this with you."

"That's ridiculous!" Lori protested.

"And why you seemed to be the object of the attacks, so that when you struck elsewhere, you wouldn't be suspected."

"This is so wrong," Jake muttered. He looked like he might make a break for the door, but the trap they were in was not physical.

"Sir, you can't believe that? You can't!" Cally was pleading.

Grant gestured to the videoscreen. "I believe in evidence."

"But that can be faked! That's not us. You must know that." Cally's disbelief was palpable.

"I'm better looking than that for a start," said Eddie.

"Film can be faked," Grant admitted, "and the guilty can lie."

"But we're being framed." Lori again. "This is insane. Can't you see that?"

"Why are you doing it? Such promising agents, too." Grant

seemed hurt now, personally spurned. "Is it because of Jennifer? Is this some sort of revenge on the school when it was you who let her die?"

Now it was Jake's turn to need restraint. "Not now," he heard Ben hiss in his ear.

"Betrayal of trust," declared Grant, "it sickens me. Take them away, Keene. I can't bear to look at them any longer."

"Mr. Deveraux!" Ben's closing gambit. "He'll believe us. We want to speak to Mr. Deveraux!"

"I have already spoken to Mr. Deveraux, Stanton," Grant revealed, "and he is of the same opinion as myself. This matter rests in my hands and my hands alone. Now take them away and lock them up, Keene, until I decide what to do with them."

Grant turned his back on Bond Team, and Ben felt his heart sinking. Nightmare. It was the only word. And somehow, he sensed that the worst was *still* to come.

CHAPTER SIX

"Will it hurt, do you think?"

"Will what hurt, Eddie?" Ben said wearily. Eddie could be trying company at the best of times, and this, the five of them cramped into the boys' bedroom with the door and window soundly locked since last night, and the hour now approaching midday, this was far from the best of times.

"The mind-wiping." Eddie wasn't going to make it any easier. "I mean, that's what'll happen, don't you think? Grant thinks we're guilty. Deveraux thinks we did it. Mind-wipe city. Farewell to the last fourteen months."

"Shut up, Eddie," Ben said, even though the same thought was lodged in his own brain like a stone in a shoe. He didn't want to face it, the possibility of everything he'd worked for, everything he'd already achieved at Spy High being taken from him, stripped from his memory like old wallpaper, as if it had never happened.

"They'd let us remember one another, wouldn't they?" Lori hoped. She reached for Ben's hand and squeezed. "They'd leave us that." Ben scarcely squeezed back.

"Well, I'm not letting anyone mess with my mind." Jake went to the window, gazed out. "Not Grant or anyone. Which means we'd better start coming up with a plan to get out of here and find out who set us up."

Cally joined him. "Look," she said, "athletics just as normal. I wonder if the others have been told about us."

"If they have, Simon Macey'll be lapping it up." Another reason for Ben to despair.

"Well, one good thing," suggested Eddie. "At least we know we were wrong about Bex."

"Yeah?" Ben snorted skeptically. "How's that, Sherlock?"

"'Cause it was a man who attacked Jake last night, that's how. And let me tell you, Bex is very much female."

"She could have an accomplice, dummy," Ben scorned. "Think about that."

"It was Grant." Cally made the announcement with such certainty that her teammates were struck into silence. "That is, if the man who had us locked up last night is Grant at all."

"What?" Eddie frowned. "You think he's a terrorist wearing a Grant mask? Guess Halloween is coming early this year."

"Think body language," Cally said. "We've all got little mannerisms, little things we do with our hands or whatever that half the time we don't even realize we're dong. Well, think about Mr. Grant. Isn't he always running his hands through his hair, particularly at tense moments?" The others gave Cally credit for her observational skills. "Yeah, so when was the last time he did that? Not last night, I was keeping count. I'm betting it hasn't been for a while, 'cause I'm betting that man's not Grant."

"A ringer," Eddie considered, almost in admiration. "Well, he had me fooled."

"A man in a duck suit'd have you fooled, Eddie," said Ben, "but if Cal's right, we're talking about a major league bad guy, someone with the resources and the daring to remove the real Grant and then replace him."

"Yeah," Jake agreed, "and it's got to be someone we know. Why else would we be the targets?"

"But who? Someone we've encountered before?" Lori ticked off a list. "Frankenstein, CHAOS, Nemesis, Talon. They're all dead or disbanded."

"What about Vlad Tepesch?" Cally said. "He's still around. Maybe out for revenge."

"It's possible." Ben's spirits were picking up now that they seemed to be making progress. "Now if we could only bypass the imposter and go straight to Deveraux. I mean, with so-called Grant in charge, how do we know that Deveraux's aware of any of this? Maybe he'll believe us."

"Great idea, Ben," Eddie applauded. "You got Big D's number? I mean, he's just so easy to contact, isn't he?"

"Well, if you've got any better —"

Lori gestured for Ben to be quiet. "There's someone at the door."

"It'll be the security guy with an early lunch," reasoned Eddie. "Who's betting on bread and water?"

But it wasn't the security guy. It was Bex. "Don't move, any of you," she said. "I know how to use this."

She was pointing a shock blaster directly at them.

IGC DATA FILE GRT 3458

. . . increased security as Graveney Westwood prepares to make history as America's first president in space. His planned inspection tour of the Guardian Star space station will allow the president to see its prodigious weaponry for himself and will include a brief official opening ceremony as the flagship of the EPI finally becomes fully operational.

At a news conference today, President Westwood, looking tanned and fit after a recent visit to a physical reconstruction clinic, dismissed out of hand criticisms from his political opponents that his imminent extra-terrestrial excursion was little more than a publicity stunt. "It's important for me to go," he said. "I want to tell all the brave men and women up there personally just how much peace-loving Americans everywhere appreciate their vigilance in keeping this little planet of ours safe from those who would destroy us. But nobody needs to worry. I'm leaving the government in good hands, and I'll be back before you know it."

In other news, manufacturers of domestic-use fallout shelters have seen sales soar . . .

"So," Ben gritted, "revealed your true colors at last, huh?"

"Ben," Bex shook her head sadly, "did you pay money to be team leader or what? If I was playing for the other team, why would I be here? You're on the way out without any help from me. Believe it or not, I am actually on your side."

She stepped further into the room, and the prostrate form of the security guard could be glimpsed unconscious in the corridor behind her.

"What did I tell you guys?" Eddie exulted. He made a move toward Bex, didn't get far before her shock blaster prodded toward his chest.

"Not so fast, Eddie," Bex cautioned. "Not yet. Get back with the others."

"Bex," Eddie complained, but the shock blaster won the argument.

"Don't you trust us?" Lori said.

"Don't you trust me?" A thin, bitter smile.

"You've given us good reason not to," Ben said. "You can't deny that, Bex."

"That's right. I can't." Bex inclined her head slowly. "Which is why I think it's time I came clean with you all. If we want to get out of this mess we're in, then we're gonna have to trust one another. No more secrets."

"We're listening," said Jake, but if he didn't like what he was going to hear, he was poised to take Bex on, blaster and all. Nobody was going to mess with his mind.

"Okay, then. Ready or not, here comes the truth. My name's not Dee. D is just its first letter, and we thought it'd make a cool kind of code name. My real name's a little longer than that. It's Deveraux." Five jaws dropping with the shock of understanding. "That's right. I'm Jonathan Deveraux's daughter."

"What?" Lori gaped. "But that doesn't make sense."

"It's the only thing that does," Jake mused.

"Oh my God," Eddie moaned. "I have a crush on the founder's daughter."

"What I told you about the substitute school is true. I've wanted to be a spy, a secret agent like the rest of you ever since I wanted to be anything. I kind of forced Dad into giving me a chance, not that he was willing. And I didn't want any strings pulled, no favoritism, so I became Dee rather than Deveraux. The teachers knew, but I didn't want my new teammates to be distracted by who my father is. I wanted them to take me at face value."

"And a very nice face it is, too," Eddie fawned, "perforations and everything. Do you think your dad'll mind if I say that?"

"Rebecca Deveraux," Cally chuckled in amused disbelief.

"Only things haven't quite turned out as planned, have they? I wasn't anticipating the rest of my team being framed for sabotage."

"So you believe we're innocent?" Lori said.

"In Eddie's case," Bex sighed sorrowfully, "as a baby. Grant's got to be mistaken."

"Worse," said Jake. "That's *not* Grant, and whoever it is has set us up himself."

"What?" Now it was Bex's turn to be shocked.

"We'll explain it to your dad. Time to break with tradition and meet the mysterious Mr. D face-to-face." Jake was eager for action. "It's the only chance we've got."

"Sorry, Jake," Bex said reluctantly. "Can't be done."

"Huh? Don't tell us you've never seen him, either." Eddie was about ready to believe anything.

"No, that's where you were going the other night, wasn't it?" Lori realized. "To your dad's rooms. I followed you. Lost you. Sorry."

"Forget it," said Bex, "but father or not, there's no way I can reach him now. Security's been upped at key locations in the school to super red. Dad's rooms have been totally sealed off, and all electronic means of contacting him are being monitored. If we've got a fake Grant and he's the danger, then he's a danger in complete control."

"So what did you come here for, Bex?" Ben spoke for the first time after a lengthy period of having apparently been deep in frowning thought. "To gloat?"

"Hardly." Grinning, Bex reached behind her, produced a second shock blaster that had been hiding in her belt. "I've got another one, too. I stopped by the armory on the way and thought they might come in handy. It's surprising how reassuring the odd shock blaster can be when you're on the run."

"On the run?" Eddie gulped.

"What else?" snorted Jake. "We can't prove our innocence and find out what's really going on by staying here and getting mind-wiped. Let me help you carry those, Bex."

"On one condition," Bex said. "I'm coming with you."

She must be thinking she's pretty clever, Ben brooded as they slunk silently through the corridors of Spy High. Turning up like that, like an armed and dangerous fairy godmother. Breaking them out. If not saving the day, then at least prolonging it. Bex Deveraux. Deveraux's daughter. Look how she was relishing the others' newfound acceptance of her, roaming ahead with Eddie. Jake and Cally on the other side of the corridor while he, Benjamin T. Stanton Jr. and Lori were relegated to the rear. At least he'd been able to take charge of the final shock blaster. A gun in his hand always made him feel better.

Jake scouted out the fire-escape stairs while the rest of them kept watch, signaled that the proverbial coast was clear. It was fortunate that morning classes were still in progress. Their fellow students would mostly be below ground, shock-suited up and carrying on as if nothing in particular was happening. If they moved fast, maybe they could SkyBike out of here without violence, although Ben for one would find a little bit of non-life-threatening violence quite therapeutic right now.

Because, while he knew he couldn't suspect Bex anymore, he was suddenly not so sure about Jonathan Deveraux himself. The founder of Spy High surely wouldn't be satisfied for his daughter to remain just another student. Ben's own father wouldn't want that for him. Surely, Deveraux had to have a promotion in mind for Bex, however mediocre an agent she was, and promotion meant team leader, and team leader was a post that was currently filled. The others might have just gained an ally, but Ben feared that he'd just acquired a rival.

They reached the ground floor. Jake hissed that someone was coming, then he was pressing back against the wall, becoming the wall. And seizing the someone. A hapless first year student. Nothing to worry about. "Sorry 'bout that," Bex apologized, dusting the boy off. "Practicing our stealth techniques, that's all. Don't tell anyone we're here, okay?" She was quick-witted as well. The others smiled. Ben didn't.

They edged outside, to the back of the mansions where there was usually little reason to go. They crouched low, scanning the scene like half a dozen CCTV cameras.

"I thought you said Mr. Look-alike had increased security," Cally whispered to Bex. Apart from a pair of distant security men who seemed to be engrossed in the even more distant athletics practice, their way appeared to be without obstacle.

"You know the one about gift horses and mouths, Cal?" Bex whispered back. "And speaking of which . . ."

A short dash away, what to a casual visitor would have looked like stables. The presence of horses peering interestedly out of their stalls would doubtlessly have confirmed that impression, unless the same casual visitor attempted to stroke their muzzle or feed them a lump of sugar. Holographic horses were difficult to pet, and they didn't need food. The stables were a disguise; the building really housed Spy High's SkyBike hangar.

"There you go," Bex laughed as they slipped inside. "Home free."

"Don't get too confident," Ben warned. "A mission's never over until it's over. You always have to expect the unexpected.

You'll learn," he added, glad for the opportunity to highlight Bex's inexperience.

For a SkyBike hangar, there seemed to be very few machines readily available. None, in fact. Bales of straw, pitchforks, and buckets occupied the floor space. Nobody seemed worried by the fact.

"Ben's right," agreed Jake, "so let's not waste time. Get ready to mount up."

He selected a hook that was set into the wall and pulled on it. A smooth electronic hum filled the air. The central area of floor began to sink beneath the ground, while at the same time, the hangar's deceptively oak-beamed roof retracted. A new floor rose up, shiny and metallic. No bales of straw for nonexistent horses now. SkyBikes. Rows of them. Sleek, glittering, and fully operational.

"I vote we take weapons-grade bikes," said Jake. "I don't plan on being caught."

"Do you think that's wise, Daly?" Like a ghost, Corporal Keene emerged from the far shadows. "I wondered when you'd get here."

"Stay where you are, sir." Ben only half-aimed his shock blaster at Keene's apparently unarmed form, and he felt somehow guilty about doing that. Lori was at his shoulder, the others bunching together. "Don't move."

Keene chuckled, advanced a little further with his open palms outstretched. "You think you can take me, Stanton?"

"There'll be no need if you just let us go," Ben bargained.

"We've been set up, Corporal," Lori added. "That's not us on that film. We're innocent."

"If I thought you were guilty, Angel," said Keene, "do you imagine I'd have even allowed you to get this far?"

"So you'll help us?" Cally asked cautiously.

"It's what I've always said," Eddie enthused. "Corporal Keene's a great guy."

"I'm afraid not," said Keene.

"It's what I've always said," Eddie groaned. "Corporal Keene's a rat."

"I have my orders," Keene pointed out, "and soldiers do as they're told."

"Doesn't that depend on who's giving the orders?" Ben pressed. "'Cause the guy giving you yours right now isn't who you think he is. Grant's the threat. He's the one who's framed us. He's a double."

Keene's lips twitched. "And I suppose you have indisputable proof to that effect?"

Ben's silence was admission that they didn't.

"Can't you just take our word for it?" Eddie hoped.

"Then I'm not at liberty to believe you," said Keene.

Jake, just as uncertainly as Ben, pointed his shock blaster at the corporal. "That's bad news," he lamented, "and not for us."

"Don't be ridiculous, Daly," Keene said dismissively, "and don't waste time. The alarm will have sounded the instant the system registered an unauthorized activation of the hangar. If you're leaving, you'd better do it now."

"But you said —?"

"I can't disobey my orders, Stanton, but I can bend them a little. Now something's wrong, I know that. You need to find out exactly what it is. I'll try to protect you from within Spy High as much as I can, but you need to prove your innocence beyond doubt before I can make any move."

"It's what I've always said," began Eddie.

"Nelligan, shut up and get out of here," Keene said with the slightest hint of amusement. "And trust to your training, all of you. You'll need to."

Ben nodded terse appreciation. "Thank you, sir." To the others: "Okay, you heard the man. We're gone!"

Swiftly now, they boarded the SkyBikes, gripped the handlebars, and gunned the engines. The magnetic power pulsed beneath them. Their chosen machines rose into the air, out into the open sky. When Lori glanced back down, Keene was already gone.

But others were arriving. Spy High's security guards, shouting for them to return, no doubt with an "or else" in there somewhere. Not that it mattered what they yelled. Bond Team wasn't listening.

"Where to?" Jake called to Ben as they headed out across the grounds.

"As far from here as possible!" Ben returned emphatically.

"Easier said than done," Eddie muttered to himself. He'd seen what lay ahead.

They headed for the woodland that encircled Spy High, and it didn't actually contain a lot of wood. It did, however, contain a significant amount of weaponry. As the school's first line of defense in case of a terrorist assault, that much was probably only to be expected. And the weapons systems could be turned inward just as easily as out. False bark split open on artificial trees to reveal the cold steel of missile launchers. Branches fanned out and became antennae, guidance systems. Laser blasters bloomed like sudden, savage fruit. Any unfortunate squirrel or bird nestling on the forest boughs was in for a shock.

"Evasive maneuvers!" Ben cried. "Grant means business."

The scorch of laser blasts blistered the air.

"Scatter! Make multiple targets!"

Stasis bolts, too. If they connected with the SkyBikes, their riders could kiss their power good-bye and pray for a soft landing.

But Bond Team had an advantage. The weapons systems were computerized, programmed, inflexible. Bond Team was quick, independent, improvisational. And Keene had been right. They could trust to their training. They were more than a match for a bit of foliage with attitude. At least, five of them were.

Ben could see that Bex was in trouble.

Her SkyBiking skills weren't as advanced as the others'. She had neither the height nor the speed necessary to elude Spy High's defenses. As her teammates raced out of range, Bex found herself caught in a crossfire, laser bolts blocking her in like bars. If only one of them struck, it would be all over for Rebecca Deveraux. Her name wouldn't help her here.

But would Ben? His own bike hovered in the air like a question. The others couldn't turn back in time. It was him or nobody. And if he left Bex behind, she wouldn't really be harmed, would she? A basic crash-landing procedure and then back to the school. Not even the imposter Grant would dare to mind-wipe a Deveraux, would he? And then she'd be out of his way, and then his position would be safe, and then . . .

And then he'd have proved himself unworthy. The team came first. At any cost.

"Evasive maneuvers," he muttered. "Forget that."

He plunged his SkyBike downward, a missile screaming toward its target; he thumbed on its weapons systems and fired. The attack trees exploded, flinging metal into the air like shrapnel. Ben's trajectory swooped him through the flames, hoisted him up again into cooler air. "He shoots. He scores!" Blowing things up *and* retaining the moral high ground. He felt good.

Bex, too. "Thanks," she called, gunning her bike toward immediate safety, "leader man."

Ben acknowledged with a noble nod of his head. But as he glanced back to check on possible pursuit, his expression grew more thoughtful. There was Spy High, receding into the distance like a memory. It was closed to him now, to all of them. They were fugitives, renegades. With a shudder of doubt, Ben wondered if they'd ever return.

"I want them found! I want them caught! I want them brought back here!" Senior Tutor Elmore Grant was not happy. A bead of almost milky sweat trickled down his forehead. He held onto the desk in his study as if his anger was physically unbalancing him. "Do you hear me, Keene?"

The surgical removal of Corporal Keene's ears would have been necessary for him not to have heard his superior's words. "Yes, sir," he responded impassively.

"Mr. Deveraux's orders, Keene. They have his daughter."

"Yes, sir."

"Then why are you still here? Dispatch a team at once. We need to act now!"

"Yes, sir," Keene gave nothing away, not the fact that he'd

spoken to Bond Team before its forced departure, not his own feelings, certainly not his own increasing suspicions. He left the study smartly and obediently.

Now he was alone, Senior Tutor Elmore Grant slumped into his chair as if overcome with sudden exhaustion. He opened a communication channel on his desk.

"Yes?" came a voice.

Grant dabbed at the sweat on his brow, rubbed the moisture slowly, pensively between his fingers, as if uncertain what it was. "Everything is going according to plan, sir," he said. "They're on the run."

"Excellent." A high-pitched giggle over the communications channel. "You have done well, my puppet."

And even though Grant addressed its owner as "sir," it was not the voice of Jonathan Deveraux.

CHAPTER SEVEN

They hadn't exactly stolen the Wheelless, just borrowed it. It belonged to Jacko's dad, in any case, so in a sort of way it belonged to Jacko, and it was the new chameleon model so it was kind of an unfair temptation, and chicks went wild for guys in a Wheelless, and what his dad didn't know couldn't hurt him. And if anyone found out, Jacko could always claim it was Donny's idea in the first place. What were best friends for if not the blame when things went wrong?

Out here, though, on the open road out in the country north of town, nothing seemed likely to go wrong. The hood was down, the breeze was ruffling their hair like a chick's fingers, and Jacko was putting the Wheelless through a test-drive. The magnetic engine hummed nonchalantly as their speed increased.

"You don't even have to keep your eyes on the road anymore," Jacko was boasting, proving it by looking anywhere but. "Object Avoidance Systems make any kind of crash impossible. An idiot could keep this baby on the road."

"You don't say," grinned Donny, setting the passenger seat for full recline. "The only thing these magnetic cars don't have is the noise. I think chicks like the revs, know what I mean? Like they've got something strong and powerful underneath 'em."

"No problem," said Jacko knowingly. "This baby's got a sound-effects suite built in. You want the authentic engine roar and screeching of tires of the old gas-driven racers? Your wish is our command. Just press 'F' for Ferrari." Jacko did. They couldn't hear themselves think, not that that thought was an occupation that had ever held much attraction for Jacko and Donny.

Girls, on the other hand . . .

"Chick alert!" Jacko indicated up ahead on the otherwise deserted roadside. She was a couple of years younger than him, maybe, but she was blond and tall and gorgeous, and she looked like she was waving them down. On his back in the passenger seat (getting in some practice, he liked to think), Donny hadn't yet noticed their sudden opportunity. Jacko turned off the sound effects. "I said chick alert!"

"What? Where?" Donny's chair sprang up so quickly it almost propelled him through the windscreen. "Wow! She wants us!"

So much for the Object Avoidance Systems.

"Play it cool. Play it cool," Jacko advised.

"She's a looker, all right," Donny declared, "but what's she doing all on her own out here?"

"I dunno," said Jacko. "Let's ask her." He pulled up alongside the blond girl, turned off the engine, and leaned in what he hoped was impressive style toward her. "Hi."

"Hi, yourself," greeted the blond. "You know, I've been waiting for someone like you to come along." She narrowed her devastatingly blue eyes seductively.

"Really?" Jacko gulped, then remembered himself. *Play it cool.* "Sure thing, babe."

"Oh, yes." The blond's slim fingers toyed with the door handle. "I wonder if you can help me. I'll be very grateful if you can."

"Yeah?" Jacko gaped.

"Grateful?" Donny gaped.

"Very," the blond confirmed, with rather more of a pant

than was strictly necessary. "I need a lift, you see, and your back-seat looks so tempting."

Jacko and Donny were out of the car as one, falling over each other, almost literally, for the right to open the rear door for the blond. Jacko got there first. "Your knights in shining armor," he said, "only without the armor."

"And we're not actually knights, either," added Donny.

The blond didn't seem to mind. "Well, well, well," she admired. "What a lot of room. You could get several people in there."

"At least three," suggested Jacko.

"What luck," said the blond, and whistled.

From hiding places behind a bank, two more girls emerged. One of them was dreadlocked and black; the other was green-haired and pierced. Both of them had a direct and debilitating effect on Donny and Jacko's knees.

"Friends of mine," the blond revealed. They waved and simpered, "Hi." "They need a lift, too."

"T-terrific," Jacko managed as the black girl pressed against him. "H-hello."

"Aren't they sweet?" Green Hair crooned as she draped herself around a trembling Donny. "And aren't they helpful?"

"For you girls," Donny groped, "anything."

"Really?" Green Hair seemed impressed.

"Really." Jacko tried to wink at Dreadlocks but it came out more like a twitch.

"Well, that's wonderful," she smiled. "We'll take you up on that."

"Hey, guys," the blond girl suddenly called. "You can come out now."

"Wha —?" If Jacko and Donny had thought the situation too good to be true, they were right. "What's going on?" As Ben, Eddie, and Jake made their appearance from behind the same bank as the girls.

"We'd like your car, please," Lori smiled, "and I'm afraid that's not really a request." There was a shock blaster in her hand.

Jacko and Donny felt the same in their ribs. "Hmm. Need to lose some weight, big guy," Bex advised.

"Thanks again, though." Cally kissed Jacko lightly on the cheek. "Don't know what we'd have done without you."

"Eddie, you drive," Ben instructed. "Cally, next to him and disengage the automatic tracer. The rest of us get to take the backseat for a while."

"It's a chameleon, Ben," Eddie said. "Want me to change the color?"

"Rotate the colors. It'll make us even harder to track."

"Ben?" said Lori. "What about Jokers One and Two?"

"Yeah, sorry, guys," Ben smiled thinly, "but look on this as a loan rather than a theft, yeah? There are some SkyBikes back there if you're up for it. Otherwise, well, I'm sure someone'll be along before dark. Tomorrow. See you around."

"Who are you guys?" Jacko stared.

"Shh!" hissed Jake. "We're secret agents, but don't tell anyone or it won't be a secret. Bye, now."

He followed the others and clambered into the Wheelless. In seconds they were out of sight, like they'd never been there.

"What are we gonna do now?" Donny pleaded.

Jacko knew what he was going to do. "This is all your fault, Donny Becker . . ."

* * *

"Okay," Eddie summarized, "so they find the bikes, they don't find us. They can't locate the car we're in. Where do you want me to point it, Ben? Stanton Towers?"

"We can't go home, Eddie," Ben said, "even if I did live somewhere with such a ridiculous name. Phoney Grant'll have someone watching our homes, you can bet on it. We don't want to endanger our parents."

"Won't he have to tell them we're missing?" Lori thought of her mom and dad, how shocked they'd be if they knew that pretty little Lori had done something as rebellious as running away from school.

"Why should he?" said Ben. "As far as they know, we're all happily boarding at Deveraux Academy. They won't necessarily start missing us until the end of term."

"And maybe not even then," Eddie remarked, as though from personal experience.

"Well, if Look-alike's staked out our homes," mused Jake, "I guess the least we can do is return the favor. We might even find some sort of clue to get us out of this mess, maybe even discover where the real Grant is. What do you think?"

"I think I've always wanted to see how our teachers live," said Ben. "Cally?"

"Already on it." She was working away furiously on the Wheelless's built-in computer. "It's too dangerous to hack into Spy High's database from here — might help them trace us — but the videophone company's got to have his details, and breaking their codes is as easy as dialing a number."

It didn't take long. Grant had an address in the Pine Glades, housing of distinction for the modern executive: remote, eco-friendly, and outrageously expensive. Cally fed the details into the car's automatic navigator. "Estimated arrival: one hour and forty minutes."

"Yeah?" Eddie grunted. "Does that time include the possibility of attack by Spy High pursuers or what?"

As it happened, Eddie's concern was irrelevant. One hour and forty minutes of uneventful travel later, he was parking the car outside Grant's house. "We're on the wrong side of the classroom," Cally was admiring. "How much do senior tutors earn?"

"Good question," said Jake, thinking of his family's meager farm and how hard his father had to work even to keep that solvent. These occasional reminders of his own impoverished background always irked him, made him feel like an outsider. He was surprised to feel Lori's hand squeezing his, comfortingly, as if she knew. "At least we know that if he's turned against us, it can't have been for money."

A copse of pines opened up to reveal the house built into the hillside and on three levels. Traditional materials had been used, no doubt to help the edifice blend in with its natural surroundings. Solar panels gleamed righteously from domed and overhanging roofs. The house looked as if it had grown out of the hillside like a clump of mushrooms, an effect the architect had no doubt intended. "I'll have a little of whatever the guy who built this was on," Eddie said. "Then I won't care what happens."

"Looks deserted," Bex observed, hopping out of the Wheelless.

"Not anymore," Jake said. "Shall we?"

"Hold on. The place is bound to be alarmed." Ben's mind ran through the various precautions they'd been taught to take before breaking and entering. He walked around the outside of the house. "Anybody see anything?"

"Got it, boss." Cally pointed to a control panel set up beneath one of the overhanging domes. She frowned curiously. "But it's green. Mr. Grant kindly didn't bother setting the alarm the last time he went out. The insurance people won't like that."

"Then they'll hate this." Lori was at the front door. Having gained her teammates' attention, she pressed her fingers against it. It swung inward. "Open."

"Right, so either Grant's got nothing worth stealing," reasoned Eddie, "or he operates some kind of weird open-door policy for anybody who just happens to be passing by, or —"

"Or he could have been abducted by persons or powers unknown," Ben gritted. "Girls, let's keep these shock blasters visible, shall we?"

Lori, Cally, and Bex led the way into Grant's hall. It opened out into a series of elegant, tastefully furnished rooms. Nothing seemed out of place, not a rug nor a cushion nor an ornament disturbed.

"No sign of a struggle," Cally said.

"Maybe there wasn't one," Lori pondered, "or maybe there was and everything's been put back the way it was before."

"Gee, I don't like his taste in art." Bex confronted a large canvas on the wall, which seemed to consist of a number of overlapping green and gray squares. "I used to do better than this in kindergarten."

"You're a genius, Bex," Ben exulted.

"No, I mean they were better, but they still weren't —"

"No, this painting. It's a twentieth-century modernist

masterpiece. Franco Odo's *The March of Man*. See, the green squares represent nature, and the advancing gray squares symbolize human civilization, which Odo sees as —"

"Hey, Professor Stanton," groaned Jake, "can we hold the lecture until we're off the dangerous renegades list?"

"Sure. Sorry." Ben shrugged. "The point is, it's hanging upside down." The others regarded him with How can you tell? expressions. "Trust me. Which means it's fallen and been put up again incorrectly. Therefore, not by Grant. Therefore, there was an intruder. And a struggle."

Lori winced. "So let's search the place and then get out of here."

"Absolutely. Three teams," Ben directed. "Me and Lori, Eddie and Bex, Jake and Cally. We'll take a level each. Note anything which might help us. Back here in thirty minutes."

"Does talking art always make him that bossy?" Bex asked Eddie.

"Ben doesn't need any excuse," Eddie replied. "You'll get used to it. The rest of us had to. Come on."

Bond Team spread out and began its investigations. Cally and Jake took the top level, the wraparound windows granting fine views of the pines and the valley below. Their focus, however, was on what was contained within the house. Bathrooms. Bedrooms. A circular room with a glass roof and a giant telescope pointed at the skies. Every room was beautifully appointed and looked more like an exhibit than an inhabited space.

"You sure he actually lives here, Cal?" Jake said. "I mean, who can possibly keep this tidy, this organized? Even the bins don't have any rubbish in them."

"That's good for us." Cally entered another bedroom, this one's size suggesting it was probably the master bedroom, Grant's own. "Means any sign of disorganization could be a clue, an indication of a presence other than Mr. Grant's."

"What, you mean like a dirty footprint or a glass not put away?"

"Exactly." Cally smiled and stooped. "Or a card left lying in the middle of the bedroom carpet." She picked the offending article up and examined it.

"Well?"

"It's a business card. 'Be Who You Want to Be'," Cally read. "'Changing Faces Physical Reconstruction Clinics.'" She thought of Grant. She thought of Lacey Bannon and of Lacey Bannon's cousin Mary, the one who for no apparent reason had gone mad in the most explosive of ways, the one whom Lacey had said had also recently visited . . . "Let's get to the others, Jake," Cally urged. "This is it."

There wasn't time.

"Attention, Bond Team. Attention!" An electronically amplified voice boomed from outside. "We know you're in there. This is Sam Miller speaking." Sam Miller. Cally knew the name. He'd graduated from Spy High several years ago, the first African-American to have led a team. Sam Miller was a trailblazer. Cally had admired his example. And now, she realized uncomfortably, she was going to have to fight him.

"They've sent a graduate team after us," Jake gritted. He crossed to the window. "We've got problems."

Sam Miller hovered in the air some twenty meters from the house, jet-packed and shock-suited, ready for action. To his right, a second figure, a redheaded girl Jake could identify as

Sheena McCulloch, another grad. Two here. No doubt the other four were detailed to Bex and Eddie, Ben and Lori.

"There'll be no need for violence if you just leave the house one at a time, and with your hands clearly visible," Sam Miller announced.

"Yeah, right," Jake muttered. "Keep that card safe, Cal. Time for some teamwork."

"We don't want to hurt you, but we're taking you back to Spy High. Mr. Grant's orders. You have one minute to start coming out, or we're coming in."

One minute, then, to organize a plan of defense.

Cally and Jake hurtled back down Grant's broad and luxurious staircase to the original rendezvous point. Ben and Lori were already there, Eddie and Bex approaching.

"Ideas?" Ben demanded. He doubted there'd be many. Three shock blasters between them and with the hillside behind, only one possible exit. The graduates were all decked out for a full-on assault, shock suits, sleepshot, etc. But there was always a way. Had to be. "Every enemy has a weakness, however strong they may seem to be." He'd read that somewhere, and it sounded good. "We only have to find it."

"In, like, thirty seconds." Eddie appeared to have appointed himself official timekeeper of Bond Team's final minute.

"We don't surrender, then," Bex hesitated.

"We never surrender." Jake's eyes blazed. "We go down fighting."

"Macho talk's no help, Jake." Cally darted to one of Grant's several expensive-looking coffee tables. She dragged it toward the center of the room, turned it onto its side. "Come on. Make a circle of these things. Give us *some* protection."

"Cal's right." Ben followed her lead. "Let's do it."

"Ten seconds," Eddie noted.

"Attention, Bond Team, I want to see you coming out now. Don't be foolish. You'll get a fair hearing. Mr. Grant has promised you that."

"Yeah, yeah," Jake scoffed. "And then a highly reasonable mind-wipe." He and Lori added a sofa to the makeshift barricade.

"Ben, don't be stupid." Sam Miller tried the personal approach. "Lead your team out. Do it now!"

"Dig in!" Ben retorted, though Miller, of course, couldn't hear him. Bond Team crouched down within their furniture stockade and awaited the attack. "Blasters to the best shots. Lori. Jake. Me." Cally and Bex handed their weapons over without complaint. Now was not the time to question the team's marksmanship rankings.

"All right," Sam Miller warned coldly. "You give us no choice. We're coming in!"

"Those without blasters keep behind those with. If somebody's hit, take over."

A shattering of glass from upstairs, in at least three locations.

"Ben," yelled Jake, "shut up and shoot!"

The door burst inward, smashed and splintered. Someone in the doorway. Ben and Jake opened fire at once. Lori didn't. Which was just as well. The first real assault came from the opposite direction and from above. Sheena McCulloch and another grad called Starkey swooped on jet-packs from the upper levels, raking the room with sleepshot. Eddie and Cally had to dive low to avoid shells hitting them and instantly terminating their interest in proceedings. At least Lori's blaster gave the grads something to think about as they circled above Bond Team like birds of prey. "Ben!" she cried.

"Watch the door, Jake!" Ben ordered, redirecting his own fire and adding it to Lori's. "Bad tactics on their part. Jet packs aren't much of an advantage in an enclosed space. I wouldn't have made that mistake."

"Mistake or distraction?" Cally punched Ben's shoulder. "Look!"

At the top of the stairs, two more grads, picking vantage points to shoot down on them. From other rooms on the same level as themselves, Sam Miller and the final member of his team racing to find cover before opening up a third front on the besieged Bond Teamers.

Ben thought bitterly of the relationship between pride and failure. Their ability to defend themselves was pathetic. They could hold the grads off for a few minutes, maybe, but sooner or later . . . If only they had more guns. If only they were wearing shock suits.

And then it came to him. As sleepshot shells ricocheted around him, as Jake let out a sudden cry, a shell striking his shock blaster and knocking it from his hand, as the graduates pressed their advantage and dared to close in. The solution. He was a genius, after all.

They were all under one roof. A roof with a sprinkler system inlaid. Grant wouldn't want any accidents in his perfect home.

"Lori!" Ben alerted. "Together! Aim for the sprinklers!"

They fired as one. The sprinklers activated, not that "sprinklers" was really an adequate word. The water that gushed from the deceptively tiny nozzles was like a deluge, a solid spray as hard and as unremitting as concrete.

It swatted Starkey and Sheena McCulloch to the floor where the former's collision with Grant's sixty-inch plasma-screen TV did not bode well for the immediate health of either.

It rammed into everybody like a wall in motion, sweeping them off their feet and sprawling.

But only the grads were wearing shock suits. And only the shock suits shorted out as the relentless water permeated their power supply. There were flashes like blown fuses, cries of pain as the suits jolted current through the trapped bodies of the wearers. Nothing fatal. Nothing even long-lived. But disorienting and debilitating enough for Bond Team to press the advantage.

Wading through water they lunged toward their attackers. No more need for shock blasters. A few well-aimed karate blows were sufficient as the graduates groveled, temporarily disabled by the electric shocks they'd suffered. Bex and Lori took out Sheena McCulloch. The two who'd been at the top of the stairs tumbled into the fists of Jake Daly. Sam Miller's companion seemed already unconscious, but the graduate leader himself was struggling to rise, his right arm wavering but looking to fire sleepshot.

"Miller's mine," Ben advanced gleefully.

"No." For the second time in as many minutes, Cally punched Ben's shoulder. "He's mine, Ben. No arguments." Her dreadlocks might have been streaked and sodden across her face, but her eyes ere clear and intense. Ben saw something in them that he'd not really noticed before. Not all pride has to do with arrogance.

"You want him, Cal, you've got him." Ben stepped aside.

Cally stood before the swaying form of Sam Miller. "I'm sorry, Sam," she said. The first African-American to lead a team.

"I really am." She chopped at his neck with the side of her hand. Without a sound, Sam Miller joined the rest of his team in oblivion. "And let me tell you, that hurt me more than it hurt you."

"Cally," Ben found himself saying, "it had to be done."

And Cally found herself regarding Ben with puzzlement. Was that sympathy in there somewhere? Was it even understanding? She wasn't able to check, because he was already turning back to the others, but it made her wonder. Maybe there were hidden depths to Benjamin T. Stanton Jr. after all.

Cally watched Lori throw her arms around Ben and kiss him extravagantly. "Great thinking with the sprinklers," the blond girl said.

"And Cally thinks we've found something important," Jake added, "don't you, Cal?"

"Yeah, well, maybe it'd better wait for a drier occasion."

"Cal's right," Ben agreed. "Let's go before reinforcements arrive. Take their sleepshot wristbands, anything we can use. One thing's for sure after this. We know we're on our own."

Eddie shook his wet head mournfully as the cascading water continued its ruination of the room. "Grant's not gonna like this," he said.

"Too bad," Ben remarked. "We don't like false accusations. Now go get the car ready, Eddie. We'll decide where we're going on the way."

"Sure, Ben," said Eddie, "but one suggestion, though."

"What?"

Eddie wrung a bedraggled sleeve. "Any chance of stopping off at the dry cleaner first?"

CHAPTER EIGHT

"We're sorry, sir." Sam Miller hung his head.

"Sorry? Sorry?" Senior Tutor Elmore Grant struggled to assimilate what the graduate leader had said. "Did you hear that, Keene?" Corporal Keene had indeed heard that, though his response was rather less excitable than his superior's. "Sorry, he says. We take them in as raw teenagers. We give them all the benefits of Deveraux Academy, we train them to be the finest secret agents ever to take the field. They graduate. They start making a name for themselves. And then what happens? Then what happens?" The six graduates continued to stare dismally at the floor of Grant's study, assuming that however many times he repeated it, the question of Then what happens? remained a rhetorical one. They were right. "We send them off on a nice, easy little mission to track down and bring back a group of recalcitrant second years — not even fellow graduates, mind you — a simple, straightforward little mission they ought to be able to complete in their sleep, and what do we get? Failure, humiliation, and what else? Oh, yes, that's it." In the simpering tones of a child: "We're sorry, sir."

Keene looked on as Grant paused for breath in his tirade, mopped his brow with a handkerchief already damp. He seemed to be sweating a lot lately. Keene could almost see little beads of perspiration at the tips of Grant's fingers, like his skin was slowly leaking. Keene didn't trust a man who sweated too much in public. In his experience, it denoted either cowardice or guilt. (And for the record, Corporal Randolph Keene had not felt the need for deodorant in nearly thirty years: Like everything else, personal hygiene was a matter of self-discipline.) Keene thought of Bond Team's continued freedom. Part of him, perhaps most of him, was glad of it.

Grant was evidently finding his second wind. "You're a disgrace to this institution, do you know that?" Keene supposed they were getting a good idea. "Maybe it's not Bond Team who should be mind-wiped after all but the six of you! Inadequate. Incompetent." His tone suddenly shifted to slyness, craftiness. "On the other hand, perhaps there is a chance for you to redeem yourselves . . ."

Sam Miller's head snapped back up. "Anything, sir. We'll do anything."

"That's good, Miller." Grant mopped his brow. Keene saw the sweat glistening. "That's so much more inspiring than 'We're sorry, sir.' Perhaps next time you encounter Bond Team, you'll do a little better."

"Next time?" Keene could have cursed himself for his unguarded interruption. "Sir?" he added quickly, kept his face impassive.

He needn't have worried. Grant did not even glance at him. "Yes, Keene. Yes, Miller. Next time. Because luckily for you, I have a very good idea where Bond Team might turn up next time, and when they do, I want you to be there to greet them. And Miller . . ." Grant growled.

"Yes, sir?"

"Next time, no mistakes."

They drove in the magnetic car as far as the city limits before dumping it and hot-wiring a new vehicle: Ben seemed to be of the opinion that the more times they changed their transport, the better, making it increasingly difficult for Grant or the graduates to locate them. The selective stealing continued when Cally disengaged the alarm system of a fashionable clothing store under cover of darkness. The following morning, the owner declared it to be the oddest theft she'd ever experienced. No money had been taken, only twelve complete sets of clothes, according to the inventory: six for teenage boys and the same number for girls. And the culprits had left the strangest of clues behind them: half a dozen water-logged outfits. She didn't know what the world was coming to.

Of course, Cally could have performed some keyboard wizardry and booked them all into the finest hotel in the city for their overnight stay, but it was decided that any kind of high profile might be dangerous. "So what kind of accommodation are we looking at to qualify for low profile?" Eddie joked. "A squat?" The others regarded him without humor. "Uh-oh. Me and my big mouth."

A squat it was, in a part of town that looked like a war zone, the few people on the streets ragged and shuffling like refugees. Cally had helped here, too. "Seeing as I spent my formative years in dives like this."

"No, this is great, Cal, really good." Eddie inspected the shell-shocked room that Cally had found for them with a kind of delighted horror. "Boarded-up windows, about thirty different types of mold on the walls, last year's vomit on the floor — I think I might move in permanently."

"It'd suit you," remarked Bex.

"It'll serve its purpose," Ben said. "We'll never be found here, so you can quit moaning, Eddie. Make the most of the breathing space. This is fine, Cally." Was that a squint, Cally wondered, or an attempt at an encouraging smile? "Now what was it that Jake said you'd found?"

"It's right here." Cally produced the Changing Faces business card and gave it to Ben. The others crowded around to see. In the squat's dim and stony light, that was a feat in itself. "Found it in Grant's bedroom. On the floor."

"With everything else racked, stacked, and neatly labeled?" Ben flexed the card suspiciously. "It's a bit Scooby Doo, isn't it? I mean, maybe it was left for us all nice and convenient."

"So what, anyway?" Bex wanted to know. "Grant's had a face-lift. What guy his age hasn't these days?"

"It's more than a face-life," Cally said. "It's a major personality change. I mean, maybe the guy in Grant's study now isn't an imposter, but the real Elmore Grant brainwashed or taken over somehow."

"Bit of a long shot on the evidence of one card, isn't it?" Bex still seemed doubtful.

Maybe it was because she was the skeptic that Ben urged, "Go on, Cal."

"Well, it's just that Lori and I heard Lacey Bannon talking the other day, and she said that her cousin had been to Changing Faces, too."

"Presumably before she went on the rampage," Eddie said.

"Hey, Eddie, you don't happen to have green eyes, do you?" From Bex.

"That's two connections to Changing Faces," Cally continued, "and two radical character transformations. That qualifies as a lead, doesn't it?"

"Lead, yes. Motive, I don't know." Ben considered. "And it

still all seems a bit too obvious. But what did the real Grant teach us back in the first term? Never overlook the obvious. I think we need to give Changing Faces the once-over, just to be on the safe side."

"The sooner the better," Eddie moaned. "Get us out of here. Hey, Bex, did you remember to pack the goose-feather pillows and satin sheets?"

"You won't need them, Eddie," said Ben. "You and Bex can take first watch. I know you like to stay up late."

"Terrific. Wonderful." Eddie slunk off to the doorway with Bex in amused pursuit. "If you were on my Christmas card list, Stanton, I'd cross you off."

Ben grinned and returned the Changing Faces card to Cally. "Guess you'd better look after this, Cal."

"Thanks." She touched the card, nearly touched his fingers. "And I'm sorry, Ben."

"Sorry?" Not understanding. "Why?"

"No servants. Guess it's not what you're used to at Stanton Towers."

He wasn't sure whether she was being mischievous or genuinely critical of his background, his wealth. He took a chance on the former. "I don't live at Stanton Towers. That was Eddie's lamebrained joke. But as for servants, what? You after an interview, Cal?"

He'd said the wrong thing. "Sure," huffed Cally. "I'm just the color for it, right?"

"No, I didn't mean it like that. I was just . . ." Ben started again. "Listen, let me tell you. We do have servants. It's the way things are if you're born a Stanton. My family, well, it used to seem to me that we owned half the world, and maybe we do."

"That must be such a drag for you," Cally said, again in an indecipherable tone.

"No. But you don't know the pressures on you to succeed, Cal, the pressures on you all the time to live up to the Stanton name, the Stanton heritage, from the day you're born. Your first word's not got to be 'mama' or 'papa' but 'winner'."

"I'm sure yours was, Ben."

"Sometimes I don't think so." Ben frowned. "At times like this, for one. I mean, what if we can't prove our innocence? What if we get caught?"

"We will and we won't," Cally said with certainty. "Your turn to listen, leader man. I don't even know who my family is. I can't remember them. All I know and all I am I learned on the street, and living on the street's got its own kind of pressure, you know? And the biggest lesson I ever learned is not to give up, to never stop trying. Trust yourself. Have faith. Because when you do, in the end things'll come right, just like they'll come right for us."

"You think so?" Ben felt strangely stirred looking at Cally.

"Sure I think so." Cally smiled knowingly. "'Cause Ben, you've got to remember one last thing."

"What's that?"

"You're still a Stanton."

Ben's laugh attracted Lori's and Jake's attention from where they were sitting side by side with legs stretched out on the floor. "Ben seems to be getting unusually chummy with Cally," Jake suggested.

"Meaning?" Lori sensed a subtext.

"Meaning, Ben seems to be getting unusually chummy with Cally." Jake's own laugh was interrupted by a wince of pain.

"What's the matter?" No subtext in Lori's concern. "Jake, are you hurt?"

"Not really. Just my hand. Bruised it when the sleepshot hit my shock blaster. Came as a shock." A line even Eddie would have scorned, though Lori's smile proved her an undemanding audience. "I'll be fine."

"Poor Jake." Lori took his hand in both of hers and stroked it gently. "When I was a little girl and ever hurt myself, my mom would always say, 'Let mummy kiss it better.' It always worked."

"Yeah? Guess you had to be pretty careful where you hurt yourself. Ah, and Lori?" Not that he wasn't enjoying her soothing ministrations. "It's actually the other hand . . ."

"Okay, I give up," Eddie was saying in the hallway, "how come, now that we're friendless fugitives slumming it in a squat, you're looking like you've just won Miss Universe — and you'd have my vote, Bex, no doubt about it. You gonna tell me?"

"You've just answered your own question, Eddie." Bex scanned the dark corridor as if almost wishing for an attack from the shadows. "It's *because* things are looking bad."

"Because?" Eddie was curious. "So does masochism run in the family, then? Is that why your dad never goes out? He's secretly a party animal so he locks himself away to enjoy the pain of loneliness?"

"Best not to mention my dad, Eddie," warned Bex, "unless you want me to go back inside and leave you here with your halitosis."

"My what?" Eddie checked he wasn't breaking out in a rash.

"It doesn't matter. Ignore me. No, the truth is, Eddie, our current shaky circumstances give me the chance to prove myself.

Me, Bex. Not Rebecca Deveraux, daughter of Jonathan Deveraux, founder of Deveraux Academy blah and umpteenth richest man in the world blah blah I bet everything's handed to her on a silver platter blah."

"Actually, Bex," admitted Eddie, "the silver platter bit sounds kind of good."

"Trust me, Eddie. It isn't." Bex turned to her teammate seriously. "There are things you don't know about my life — things you don't want to know."

"Really? But I want to know everything."

Bex grinned and returned her gaze to the corridor. "That's what I like most about you, Eddie," she chuckled. "You're such a joker."

Only Eddie hadn't been joking.

It was decided next day that only Jake and Cally should visit the Changing Faces clinic whose address was on the card. "All six of us turning up might seem a bit like overkill," Ben explained. "We'll go for the split-team strategy."

"So why Cally and Jake?" Eddie grumbled. Perhaps a little unrealistically, he'd been hoping for Bex and himself. "You've gone for those most in need of physical reconstruction, right?"

"Another crack like that, Eddie," Jake returned, "and you'll be needing some physical reconstruction yourself. Starting with your nose."

"All right, all right, let's start the day with some maturity, okay?" Ben clearly wasn't in the mood for banter. He'd slept badly and was sure his bones would never be the same shape again. "Cally's in, in case there's a chance to access their data files. Jake's in, in case there's a chance of violence. Not that either of you should do anything stupid at this stage. Keep to your cover story and just check out their operation. Drop a few hints, maybe. For all we know, we could be heading one way down a blind alley."

To begin with, it certainly looked like it. The only suspicious feature about the façade of the Changing Faces clinic was its total lack of suspicious features. The broad, black, one-way glass of its windows, the gold-gleaming lettering of its name, even the polished marble steps leading up to its automatic-door entrance — all were eminently respectable, even refined. If the clinic were a person, it would be a member of all the most conservative clubs in the city, a patron of the arts, and would work fashionably late in the evenings before going home to its wife.

Jake hated it before he'd even stepped inside.

There was an elegant reception area that seemed to be doubling as a botanical garden, and judging by the number of people sitting waiting with varying degrees of patience, business was booming. Small surprise, thought Cally, casting her eye over the clinic's clients. It was in their faces. Depression. Despair. The knowledge of failure. The desperate desire for something they felt they deserved. A change. Little lost people in a big inexplicable world. Cally remembered the Changing Faces slogan: "Be Who You Want to Be." She certainly knew who she didn't want to be. And where. Maybe Ben had been wrong to assign her to this task, after all. Too late now. Jake was already talking to the receptionist.

"No, I'm afraid we don't have an appointment," he was saying. "This is really a kind of spur-of-the-moment thing. You know, buying a treatment for my uncle as a birthday gift. He's not so steady on his legs these days, Uncle Vinnie, is he, Cal?"

Cally agreed that Uncle Vinnie's Olympic sprinting days were behind him. "A new lower body'd do him good."

"I'm afraid Dr. Scarletti — she's our resident therapy and treatment adviser — I'm afraid she doesn't see anyone without an appointment." The receptionist, a girl not much older than the members of Bond Team, with wide worried eyes and apparently devoid of color, did not hold out a great deal of hope.

"Dr. Scarletti, she's in charge? She sees all the clients?" Jake established. "And she's been here awhile, has she?" Since the clinic opened, apparently. "Then she might know a friend or ours. It was him who recommended we come here. Name of Elmore Grant."

The receptionist seemed uncertain what to do with the information.

"Could you do us a favor?" Jake raised his most winning smile. The receptionist, rather timidly, seemed to respond. "You're the only one who can help us. Could you maybe buzz through to Dr. Scarletti and mention that two friends of Elmore Grant are here? Jake Daly and Cally Cross. I'm sure she'll be interested, maybe even fit us in between her other appointments."

"That's rather irregular," the receptionist wavered.

"Please? We'd really appreciate it." Jake leaned further forward, dark eyes pleading. "*I'd* really appreciate it."

For the first time, a spot of color on the receptionist's cheeks. "I'll see what I can do. Take a seat, please."

They did. "I'm impressed," Cally conceded. "She's actually doing it."

"The old animal magnetism," Jake said nonchalantly, blowing on his nails. "Works every time."

"She's smiling at you. I don't believe it."

"Some girls simply have good taste, that's all." Jake grinned. "Listen, I think I'm gonna go talk to her some more. If she's been here awhile, maybe she can tell us something."

"What, like her phone number?"

The receptionist hadn't been there awhile, and she wasn't planning on staying much longer, either. Jake thought he saw her shudder. Intrigued, he asked why. "Oh, no reason," the girl said, too nervously for that to be the case. "Nothing, really. It's just, well, you sometimes get the sense that things are strange here, that strange things are going on, you know, in the background, where you're not supposed to notice them."

"What sort of strange things?" Jake struggled to keep his tone casual, but he knew that Cally had been right. Somehow, Changing Faces was the key.

"Oh, nothing I can talk about here. That wouldn't be right."

"Well, what if I meet you after work? What time do you finish?"

The receptionist regarded Jake quizzically. "Why are you so interested? I don't understand. Who are — Dr. Scarletti!"

Jake turned to see the approach of a tall, bony, haughty woman, a woman who might conceivably have benefited from the services of her own clinic. From the direction of the receptionist's paralyzed stare, he guessed that this was Dr. Scarletti. He didn't have a clue who the burly bruisers accompanying her were, but their purpose seemed clear enough. Jake tensed his muscles.

"Miss Benson —" Dr. Scarletti's voice was like a sizzle of acid — "you are not employed to gossip with inappropriate young men. Kindly point out Jake Daly and Cally Cross for me."

Hearing her name, Cally got up and joined Jake by the reception desk.

"Dr. Scarletti, this is Jake Daly," the receptionist indicated, "and Cally Cross."

"Pleased to meet you, Dr. Scarletti." Jake extended his hand. The doctor regarded it as if it were something poisonous.

"I understand that you claim I might be acquainted with a friend of yours." Dr. Scarletti's vaguely revolted expression implied unhappiness with this possibility.

"That's right," Jake said. "A Mr. Elmore Grant. He's been here for treatment."

"I'm afraid he has not," asserted Dr. Scarletti. "There is no Mr. Elmore Grant on our records, and I have never heard the name before this morning. You are mistaken."

"Really?" Jake's disbelief was clear. "Well, thanks for leaving your patient so promptly and gathering up the hired help and everything just to tell us you've never heard of the guy. What would we get if you did know him? The red carpet?"

Dr. Scarletti smiled thinly. "My colleagues are here to escort you from the premises. We do not have what you are looking for, I am afraid, and I think you should go now. Oh," as an afterthought, "and don't come back."

Dr. Scarletti turned sharply and stalked back toward the inner recesses of the clinic. Her hulking companions did not. They shuffled grinningly closer to Jake and Cally. If their knuckles had scraped along the floor, they couldn't have looked more like gorillas.

"You boys gonna throw us out?" Jake challenged. "Think you're up to it?"

The low chuckle in their throats certainly suggested they'd give it a try. Jake braced himself.

"No," Cally hissed, clamping his biceps like a prison warden. "No violence, Ben said. We leave nice and politely." *For now,* she thought.

Jake was surprised to find that the receptionist had also been galvanized into action and was now standing at his other shoulder. "Please," she said, "no trouble."

"Hear that?" Jake addressed the neanderthals. "I always listen to the ladies. Looks like you boys have just been spared a beating."

The receptionist was at his ear. "Eight o'clock," she whispered. "I have to work late. Meet me outside at eight o'clock. I'll tell you —"

"Miss Benson." Dr. Scarletti spoke from where, unnoticed, she'd been observing the scene. "Kindly return to your duties, please."

"Bye, then, Dr. Scarletti!" Jake called. He was happy to leave now. He was happy for the receptionist to go back to her desk. He'd be seeing her again.

But eight o'clock came and went and no receptionist appeared outside the clinic. It had been thought sensible for only Jake and Cally to make the rendezvous initially, so as not to overwhelm the girl. Their teammates were thirty minutes behind them. Therefore only Jake and Cally were growing restless and puzzled as they loitered on the other side of the street and watched the minutes pass.

"She's late." Jake was shaking his head darkly. "Something's wrong."

"You think she didn't just forget? Or change her mind?" Cally grinned. "Women have been known —"

"No, she wanted to talk. Something's wrong." Jake was adamant.

"Maybe she said inside."

"She said outside, but there's no harm in checking, I guess."

Together, they crossed the empty street and, for the second time that day, approached the entrance to the Changing Faces clinic. For the second time, the doors whisked obligingly open. For the second time, they went in. The reception was deserted now, and only the building's night-lights were on, but for the second time, they saw Miss Benson at her desk, as wide-eyed and worried as before. It was surprising that she didn't seem to notice them.

"Hey, it's us. Jake and Cally." Jake advanced toward her. "Thought you said you'd . . ." His voice trailed off uneasily. "Oh, no. Oh, no . . ."

"Jake, What . . . ?"

It was little wonder that the receptionist hadn't remembered to meet them outside. She wasn't going to be remembering anything anymore. In her neck was the mark of a hypodermic needle.

"Cally, she's dead."

CHAPTER NINE

Cally drew her shock blaster. The sleepshot wristbands she'd removed from the graduates gleamed. Tonight, they'd come prepared. "Are you sure?"

"I know a dead girl when I see one," Jake said bitterly. "I've handled enough of them." He remembered a fateful night mere months ago. Undertown, LA. A squealing car. A body thrown. Jennifer, cold in his arms. As cold as Miss Benson now, as he eased her to the floor and closed her sightless eyes. "I didn't even know her first name."

"We ought to get out of here, wait for the others." Cally's vision drilled into the darkness of the inner clinic, alert for movement of any kind. "We might not be alone."

"No," Jake refused. "She died because Scarletti saw her talking to us. We're not just letting that go to waste. I'll keep watch, Cal." He drew his own shock blaster. "You get on the computer and find out something that can help us, anything that links Grant to this place. We're not leaving empty-handed."

"I'm on it." Cally quickly settled herself at the console. Give her a computer to play with, and her confidence always soared. Nobody could match her. She bypassed the system's security with the ease of avoiding pedestrians on the sidewalk. "And here we go," she announced.

Jake, meanwhile, was edging further toward the corridor that must lead to consultation rooms, offices, any operating theater that the clinic might have — rooms that might reward exploration. The corridor looked enticing, innocent, like the cheese in a mouse trap. Jake was not tempted. He covered the corridor with his blaster and waited for Cally to do her work.

"I'm scanning the list of Changing Faces' clients," she said. "The national database. There are so *many* of them."

"Is Grant there?"

Cally scrolled through the Gs. "Yes, he's here. Grant, Elmore. Male. The clinic's code number."

"Anything else?"

"Not on Grant, but wait a second. I want to check something. Mary Bannon."

"Okay." What was that? For a second, Jake had averted his gaze from the corridor, and in that second, hadn't something just moved down there? He gripped his gun more tightly.

"She's here, too, Bannon, Mary. Same info as for Grant, only —" puzzlement — "she's got two code numbers. Actually, so have a lot of them."

"Maybe they've been treated at two different clinics."

"It's likely," Cally considered, then her fingers flew across the keyboard. "Jake, I'm going to try something. I'm saving a list of dual-coded patients, then I'm going to cross-reference the names with the police files we were taught to hack into last term."

"Any reason, Cal? Other than to demonstrate your alarming computer skills once again. Only I've got a feeling someone knows we're here." The air in the corridor seemed to be trembling, like it was concealing a predator about to pounce.

"Mary's dual-coded and went crazy. There've been lots of unaccountably violent actions by previously perfectly ordinary people lately. Futurephobes. The police files have the names of everyone involved. I'm just wondering . . . Oh, my God . . ."

"What? What?" Jake was torn between keeping watch on the corridor and turning to Cally, who was staring with almost uncomprehending horror at the computer screen.

"They match. The lists match. Every single person who's freaked out in the last three months has been a dual-coded client at Changing Faces. And if I run a search on this second code number . . . You were right, Jake. It's another clinic, a hospital upstate. Everyone on the list's been there. I'm downloading the details now."

"Print them off quickly," Jake said. "I thought I heard . . ." Something. It sounded like knowing laughter, if that was possible. From the deepest reaches of the clinic.

"Everyone," Cally was saying. "They're converting their clients into psychos, making them paranoid, turning them into time bombs."

It was someone giggling, or the ghost of someone giggling. Jake strained his ears. The sound seemed chillingly familiar. "Cally . . ."

"From Aaronivitch, Ephraim to . . . oh, no, that is not good."

"What's not good? Talk to me, Cal."

Why had the giggling stopped?

"Westwood, Graveney. Male. Dual-coded. Procedure carried out at . . . Jake, they've been working on the president!"

The explosion was muffled, modest, like it was too shy to want to draw attention to itself. But the sudden flare of the fireburst at the far end of the corridor rather gave it away. And it flamed toward the teenagers like a blazing comet. "Incoming!" Jake had time to yell. "Down!"

He dived. Headfirst. The fireball seared above his head like instant sunstroke, continued on its way. Cally ducked beneath the reception desk, grabbed for the computer printout and stuffed it unread into her jacket. The fireball crashed against the window like a wave against the rocks, the flames spreading, growing. There were smaller, subsidiary explosions now, too, at strategic intervals encircling the students. A ring of fire.

"It's a trap!" Jake bounded to his feet, crossed to Cally. "We've been suckered in!"

"Then let's sucker out again!" Cally shoved Jake toward the door.

Which this time did not open, obligingly or any other way. They were pressed as tightly together as a spy's lips during interrogation.

The heat was rising. Jake felt his shirt clinging to his body like a frightened child. "Blast them!" he cried. "Together."

The shock blasters fired. They scorched but did not penetrate the glass of the doors.

"Where's Keene with his pulse rifle when you need him?" Jake cursed. "Try the windows! Now!"

Same effect. Little effect. The windows smoked blacker than their one-way glass, but they did not shatter, they did not yield. And the fire was groping across the carpet toward them like innumerable nicotine-stained fingers.

Cally glanced at it anxiously. "The others'll be here soon, won't they?"

"They'd better be," sweated Jake, "or it won't be worth them coming at all."

Plants flared brightly, briefly, and crumbled into ash. Computer screens quivered like they were about to burst into tears, their innards melting like electronic ice cream.

Then Cally was pointing at the windows and crying out in triumph: "Look!"

Ben and the others. They couldn't see her or Jake, but they probably could make out the raging inferno around them. Lori was trying the door, shouting her failure to Ben. He was snapping orders.

The flames seemed to make a grab for Jake and Cally. "Move it, Ben!" Jake bellowed, "Cal, get ready!" He saw his teammates lining up, leveling their shock blasters at the window. "Aim for the same spot! Maybe six blasters'll do what two can't!"

Bond Team fired. The window burst in a spray of jagged shards, cold air flooded in, and the fire writhed in it. Flames still hung between Jake and Cally and freedom like burning curtains, but they could see Ben, Eddie, Bex, and Lori, all shouting for them to come on, to leap through. Jake found Cally seizing his hand. "What are we waiting for?"

They hurtled for the flames. Covered their eyes with their forearms. Launched themselves at the gaping hole in the window.

A blistering pain. A sense of roasting. Then they were sprawling on the cold concrete, and their teammates were around them, expressing concern, helping them up.

"What happened?" Ben wanted to know.

"They killed the receptionist," Jake said. "They knew we were coming."

"But have we got some information for you." Cally drew out the crumpled computer printout.

"What is it?" Bex asked.

"The way forward," Cally said. "I think it's time we all went to the hospital."

"Welcome," smiled the tour guide, "to the only dedicated, purpose-built physical reconstruction hospital in the country. Owned and operated by Changing Faces, this state-of-the-art facility really is where you can become who you want to be." She laughed prettily and wrinkled her little nose, tossed her auburn hair. She stroked slender fingers down flawless cheeks. "You'd never believe I'm actually seventy years old, would you? No? Well, it's true. I have grandchildren of eight and ten and I'm dating a young man of twenty-four. That's what Changing Faces treatments can do for you, ladies and gentlemen." Spontaneous applause and gasps of approval from the gathered ladies and gentlemen, a group of about thirty. "And that, of course, is why you've come here today: to be shown just some of the secrets behind the Changing Faces name and hopefully to reassure some of you that if you choose physical reconstruction to improve your lives, then you'll want to choose Changing Faces. Now, if you'll follow me, please, our tour can commence."

More applause. Excited murmurs. The group eager to follow as the guide led them through the hospital's glass-walled atrium and toward its treatment centers.

"This is great, isn't it?" said a man to the blond boy beside him, a man whose sizable girth hinted at why he might be on the tour.

"Yeah. Really great," said Ben, the irony of his tone apparently lost.

"You're supposed to be smiling, Ben," Lori whispered. "Everyone else is."

"Everyone else is a moron," Ben snapped back, but displaying his teeth as he did so. Lori was right, of course. They had to look the part, had to play the avid visitors to the hospital, or they might draw unwanted attention to themselves. They'd be taking care of their real business soon enough. He glanced across to Eddie and Bex who were also on the tour but who seemed as oblivious to the presence of Ben and Lori as they would be to total strangers. That was part of the pretense, too. Keep with their immediate partners. If one pair failed, another might succeed. Jake and Cally, of course, couldn't infiltrate the hospital this way — they might have been videotaped or something at the clinic. They were finding their own way in. Ben only wished he was with them.

Lori seemed to sense his discontent. "It'll be all right," she encouraged.

He hoped so. Maybe they should have tried contacting Keene or going to the police, as Eddie had suggested. He hoped he hadn't rejected those courses just because Eddie's suggestions came with a tradition of disaster. But no, they wouldn't have worked. Messages were too easy to intercept, and Grant probably had the authorities in his pocket. No, they had to persevere on their own. The truth about Grant and their own framing, about the red list and those outbreaks of violence, about (potentially most worrying of all) the link between Changing Faces and the president, the truth had to be here, somewhere. Ben knew it. And he'd do whatever was necessary to find it.

* * *

"Cally, how are we doing with the door?"

In an area of the hospital where the guided tour never went, an outside area that none of the patients' bedrooms overlooked, a place of waste storage and sealed entrances, Jake and Cally were breaking in. Jake brandished a take-no-chances shock blaster and scanned for possible interruptions while Cally worked on the lock.

"Nearly there," she informed him. "You can tell they're hiding something in here. A normal hospital would never have this level of security. But then, I guess a normal hospital wouldn't have this caliber of intruder, either. Ta-daah!" The door clicked open. "This way please, ladies, gentlemen, and secret agents on the run."

"If I wasn't on duty, I could kiss you, Cal."

They both grinned. But in the doorway, with the unknown stretching before them, Cally paused. "Jake, the clinic was a setup, wasn't it, a trap? What if this is, too? What if we're walking right into it, all of us? What if they wanted us to come here?"

"You worry too much about the what-ifs and you get shot where you stand," Jake said. "Whatever might be in here waiting for us, we've got no choice. We've got to go on."

Cally nodded, consented. Keeping close together, they crept into the hospital.

As they moved out of sight of the doorway, the air rippled, like a pool disturbed by a breeze. The ripples molded themselves into two human forms, solidified into bodies. The expressions on the faces of Sam Miller and his fellow grad were grave.

Lori couldn't help remembering the book she'd read as a child, a twentieth-century classic, apparently, something about a chocolate factory. She couldn't think of the lead character's name, but she did recall that he visited a strange and marvelous chocolate factory where bizarre things having to do with making candy went on in every absurdly named room. The Changing Faces hospital seemed to be pretty similar, apart from the absolute absence of confectionery products.

Take the room they were in now, for example. The Facial Remolding Center. Great glass cases of nutrient solutions with flesh like a potter's clay growing in them. And on one whole wall, a cabinet of faces, eyeless, lifeless — masks with the high cheeks and the perfect noses that would form the template of the patient's improved appearance. Then there, the bank of leather recliners, rich red (so as not to show the blood?), in which the patients would rest while the surgery was performed. Up to ten clients could be treated at any one time, the tour guide boasted, and all to the highest standards of workmanship, thanks to the unparalleled quality of the surgical equipment that was available at Changing Faces. Lori assumed she was referring to the glittering arrangements of knives and scalpels and what looked like potato peelers that were suspended above each of the recliners. They made a dentist's surgery look like Santa's workshop. If a torturer had received a collection of such instruments as a Christmas present, he'd have been a happy man. What some people would endure in the name of vanity! The Facial Remolding Center made Lori feel queasy.

Which was something of a bonus. It might actually improve her performance. She doubled up suddenly and slapped her hand over her mouth as if she was going to be sick. "Oh, Ben!" she groaned.

Ben held her. She seemed to have developed stomach

cramps. "Ah, excuse me. Excuse me! Miss!" He signaled to the tour guide. "My girlfriend, she's not well."

"Then she's in the right place," joked a boy from the other side of the group. *Don't overdo it, Eddie,* thought Ben.

The tour guide, in the middle of her spiel about the wonders of facial remolding, did not seem to relish the interruption. "Oh, well. If the rest of you wait here for a moment I'll escort —"

"It doesn't matter," Ben responded smartly. "You carry on. I can take her back to the atrium myself. I remember the way."

"Very well. Then perhaps you can rejoin the tour later. We still have the repigmentation area to see." *Yeah,* thought Lori. *And the rack. And the thumb screws.*

But it was good that the guide preferred to continue rather than accompany the two of them back to the hospital's atrium. Because that wasn't really where they wanted to go. No sooner had Ben helped an ailing Lori out of the Facial Remodeling Center and out of everybody's sight than her health seemed to stage a comeback of Lazarus proportions.

"Okay. Good," approved Ben. "Now let's find out what there is to see that's off the tourist trail." He pointed. "She hurried us past that corridor quickly enough."

"No signs telling us what's down there," Lori observed, "unlike everywhere else."

"Then I don't know about you, Lo," said Ben, "but my interest is piqued."

They moved briskly into the unidentified corridor, eyes sharp, senses alert. But even if they did encounter a doctor or a member of the hospital staff who might question their presence there, they were only members of the tour group who'd lost their way. As it happened, though, they reached the end of the corridor without seeing anyone. Before them was a pair of sliding doors: AUTHORIZED PERSONNEL ONLY.

"After you?" said Ben.

"What, you can't read?" A female voice seemed to float out of thin air. Ben and Lori whirled. "In what sense are two renegade students from Spy High authorized personnel?" The air was rippling again. It parted to make way for four new arrivals.

"Damn," cursed Ben, as Sheena McCulloch and three of her team surrounded them. They held stunners. SPIEs. He gazed resentfully at the surveillance and protection invisibility emitters that encased the left forearms of the four graduates. "No fair."

"You wouldn't believe it," Lori began innocently. "We were on this tour of the hospital, see, and . . ."

"You think Ben and Lori have had long enough?" Eddie whispered to Bex. Then, with sufficient volume for all to hear: "This is great, isn't it?"

"I've certainly had enough of this. It's bone grafts next, didn't she say? That I can do without." Bex urged Eddie on. "Our turn."

Eddie stopped dead, regarded his feet with horror. "Oh, dear, my shoelace has come undone. I'd better tie it up again, or I'll be tripping over it. Excuse me. Sorry." He knelt down while the rest of the group carried on regardless.

"Eddie," hissed Bex. "Those shoes don't have laces."

"They don't know that," Eddie hissed in return. And louder again: "You might need to help me here, babe. I seem to have got in a tangle."

Bex dropped alongside her teammate as the tour group ahead turned a corner.

"I'll tangle *you* one of these days, Eddie."

"Yeah? Promises, promises. Listen," standing up, "I saw a PRIVATE sign back there. That'll do for a start. Come on."

"I don't know what to say." Dr. Scarletti compensated by shaking her head bemusedly. "When your Mr. Grant contacted me this morning to warn of these anarchist saboteurs who were planning on doing damage to our great hospital—" she indicated the captive and glowering Ben and Lori — "naturally, I didn't believe him at first. Could there be such twisted minds in the world, I asked myself."

"You should know!" snapped Lori. "You've got one. You killed that receptionist. You led us here!"

"Quiet, Lori!" Sheena McCulloch ordered. "This nonsense isn't helping."

"They're playing you for a fool, McCulloch," warned Ben. "All of you. You've got to listen to us. Grant's *involved* . . ." How could they have ever graduated when they were this stupid? Maybe Spy High's intake had been weak that year. Ben resigned himself to a sullen silence. There wasn't much he and Lori could do here in Dr. Scarletti's office. Best to watch and wait.

"Well, it seems now that I should be grateful to Mr. Grant," the doctor was continuing. "Who knows what havoc these two reprobates might have caused roaming unchecked through the hospital?"

Scarletti must have traveled here directly from the clinic, Ben reasoned, to be ready for them. She must have guessed that the fire wouldn't claim Jake and Cally. The information they'd found there had been meant to be found. It was a lure, a promise, to get them here, to the hospital. But why? Someone was playing games with them. Who?

"And of course," said Scarletti sweetly, "I'm grateful to the four of you young people as well, and your wonderful gadgets! I must give you a reward before you go."

"There's no need for that," said Sheena McCulloch.

"Oh, I think there is," said Dr. Scarletti. "Every need." She rummaged in her desk. "And here it is now."

Lori saw her eyes glitter madly. "Run!" she yelled.

The grads didn't even have time to move. Dr. Scarletti wielded her own stunner with unlikely expertise. She fired four times.

The grads were unconscious before they hit the ground.

"Well," said Dr. Scarletti briskly, "no more need for pretense. Come with me, please, Ben and Lori." An enigmatic smile. "There's someone who'd like to renew your acquaintance."

Jake and Cally knew they were getting somewhere when the lights turned red. "Off-limits red," as Keene had termed it back at school. They clung to the shadows as an armed and uniformed guard patrolled past. Jake indicated the way he'd come, and they stole forward stealthily.

"It'd be easier if we had radar vision capacity," complained Cally.

"It'd be easier if we had the faintest idea what we're supposed to be looking for." Jake struggled not to let the tension get the better of him.

"We're thinking maybe mind control or something? Then what about in here?"

It was some kind of lab, for experimentation or research purposes. The exact nature of the work carried out there neither Jake nor Cally could guess, but they had a pretty good idea of its general direction. All around them, mounted on and monitored by banks of computers, human brains bubbled in vats of chemicals, like clumps of meat being boiled.

"I think you might be on to something, Cal," said Jake.

"Are these real brains?" Cally winced. "I mean, did they used to be in people's heads?" She felt her own skull instinctively, as if to check it was still intact.

"Maybe we'll get some answers over here." Jake had seen a screen above a videoplayer. A disk was available to play. Jake switched the machine on.

Cally nearly brought up her breakfast. "Oh, my God, that's disgusting!"

The film bore the simple caption PROCEDURE 341: BRAIN IMPLANT. It showed the procedure taking place, in sticky scarlet close-up. Thin, sharp metal instruments probing at the bulging gray lobes of a brain, a brain whose protective skull had been sliced off like the top of an egg.

"Turn it off, Jake, please," begged Cally. "Internal organs and me really don't —"

"Yeah, Jake, turn it off," said the voice of Sam Miller. "And don't even think about your shock blasters. I'm afraid you're both pretty much covered."

To prove the point, Sam Miller and his teammate materialized. They held stunners that were pointed at Jake and Cally's chests with can't-miss accuracy.

"You know what's coming next, don't you?" Sam tested.

"Drop our weapons?" Jake ventured.

"And I'd heard you weren't big in the gray matter department."

"You're the one who needs his brains tested, Miller," growled Jake. "Maybe you've come to the right place. If you just listen to us —"

"Blasters. Drop them. Now."

Jake and Cally glanced at each other. They didn't seem to have a choice. The clatter of weapons on the metal floor did not release the tension.

"That's good," said Sam Miller, "and maybe I'll listen after we get back to Spy High."

"No, it's got to be now," Jake urged. "We're innocent. We didn't do anything. Grant's either an imposter or under some kind of mind control. He's framing us. Look at the screen, Miller. Brain implants. That's what they're doing here. For all we know, they've done one on Grant!"

"You're lying," judged Sam Miller.

"We're not!" Cally was hurt that he of all people should think so. "You've got to believe us, Sam. Look around you. See for yourself. There's something evil here. Sam, *think* for yourself!"

And maybe Cally might have gotten through. For a second, a doubt seemed to crease Sam Miller's forehead. But then, totally without warning, the lights went out.

"What?" The grad leader instinctively let off a shot. Jake had already moved.

"Cal!" he snapped. "Out of here!" He didn't know why the lights had failed, but he sure wasn't going to stick around to find out. He bunched his muscles to barrel into Miller and send him sprawling.

Someone got there first.

In the darkness, a blur of speed. Fists and feet in violent harmony. Cries of pain from the graduates, a futile stun blast ricocheting from the ceiling.

Cally was at Jake's side. "Is it one of us?"

"I don't think so," said Jake, whose skin was crawling, whose breath was quickening. He didn't know why.

A single figure now stood before them, a silhouette, a shadow. Their height. Their size.

Is it one of us?

"Oh, my God," gasped Jake as the lights were somehow restored.

Because, in a way, it was.

"Guess what?" said Eddie. "I'm starting to wonder if this place has actually got any authorized personnel. I mean, that'd explain the lack of conversation in the corridors." Since they'd sneaked into the prohibited area, he and Bex had seen no one, either any of their teammates or hospital workers of any description. "Do you think there's been an evacuation or something, and we've missed it?"

"I think you spoke too soon," Bex cautioned from a few feet ahead of Eddie, "and why doesn't that surprise me?" She pressed herself against the wall, peeked again around the corner they'd come to. "Check out Mr. Guard Duty 2062."

Eddie stole his own sneak preview of what the turning had to offer, taking care to kind of rub up against Bex where she couldn't protest. A guy had to grab his chances when he could. "No worries," he whispered, assimilating the single pulse-rifled guard outside an intriguingly closed door. "We can take him if we need to. Do you want to do it or should I?"

"I tell you what, let's draw straws, make it exciting."

Eddie was about to respond, but Bex hushed him. There was activity at the door. Somebody was coming out of the room beyond. A woman in a white coat and carrying a tray of plates piled with the remains of a half-eaten meal. "Not too hungry today," she informed the guard.

"Being a prisoner must do something to your appetite," joked the guard.

The woman smiled thinly and went on her way, which was fortunately in the opposite direction to Eddie and Bex.

"Prisoner?" Bex mused. "Any captive of theirs must be an ally of ours, right?"

"Sounds reasonable," agreed Eddie. "Whose in the need for some jailbreaking?" He rummaged in his pocket, produced a small, rounded stone.

"What are you doing, Eddie? Is that some kind of mini-bomb or quick-release gas grenade or something?"

"Bex, I know you're up on the secret agent stuff," said Eddie tolerantly, "but it's a stone. Sometimes technology just gets in the way. Watch this."

As the guard inclined his head to consult his watch, Eddie threw the stone as far as he could down the corridor. It clacked against the floor, and the guard automatically turned to face the direction of the sound. "Who's there?" he said, with a scandalous lack of imagination.

"We are!" Eddie supplied, barreling into the man from behind. "Which is bad news for you." A single karate chop was all that was required. "I think you can forget the bonus this week."

Bex retrieved the guard's pulse rifle. "Just in case you run out of stones, Eddie."

They eased the door to the prisoner's room open gently, carefully, like they were handling volatile explosives. The room was in darkness, bare of furniture but for a single chair alongside what could have been a psychiatrist's couch. The figure that writhed and wriggled on the couch at the sight of Eddie and Bex, however, had not volunteered for therapy, it seemed. Even in the dark, they could tell he was bound and gagged. When Eddie turned the light on, they could tell a little more as well.

"Mr. Grant!" The students gaped at each other. "So the other one *is* an imposter."

"Then we'd better set the real one free," Eddie said. "Come on, I'm not good with knots."

Eddie would have thought Senior Tutor Grant would have been pleased to see them, but his eyes were still wild and his expression desperate. Didn't he want to be rescued? "It's okay, sir," Eddie reassured him. "We'll have you out of here in a second. What's that? Let me get your gag."

"Behind you!" Grant screamed.

The room seemed suddenly full of guards. They all had guns. "Take it real slow, kids," one of them said. "It's the end of the line for you."

The figure walked toward them. A girl, very much their own age. A girl who was smiling subtly, knowingly.

"No." Jake's throat was thick. He could scarcely talk. "It's not . . . possible . . ."

The girl's hair: long, black, luxuriant. Her eyes: green like a cat's. Her Asian features perfect and without blemish. Lithe limbs clad in what seemed to be a shock suit. Four months ago, the sight of Jennifer Chen approaching Jake, Cally, or any other member of Bond Team would have gone without comment. Four months ago, Jake would have wanted her near him more than anything.

But that was four months ago. Before Jennifer Chen died.

Before she was buried.

"Jen, is it you?" For Jake, the rest of the world was suddenly swimming out of focus, a dream, an irrelevance. The world was a square meter of space, with him in it and Jennifer in it and his sanity slipping. "Is it really you?"

"It's really me, Jake." The green eyes sparkled but they were hollow eyes, Jake felt. And he felt that something was missing from them. "I've come back. I couldn't let them take you, could I? I couldn't let them hurt you. And do you want to know why?"

"What? Jen, I don't . . ." He put his hands out to touch her, to steady himself. She stepped backward. Jake floundered.

"So I can hurt you myself!" The words were thrown in his face like acid.

And it was the words that sent him spinning, falling, not the kick. He sought unconsciousness gratefully, the security of oblivion. The last thing he saw was Jennifer's cruel gloat of triumph.

And Bond Team's future was down to Cally.

"Jennifer," she gasped, as her former teammate stood over Jake's unmoving body, "what are you doing?"

"Anything I tell her to do, my dear." A second voice, male this time, and like the memory of an old nightmare. Cally turned to face its owner. The high-pitched giggle gave his identity away even before it was confirmed by sight. The awkward angular body. The leering, ugly face. The death-white hands and the oozing toothpaste fingers. He stepped forward, flanked by armed guards.

If her mind had been rational at this point, a number of things might suddenly have seemed clearer to Cally Cross. As it was, she couldn't think at all.

"Dr. Averill Frankenstein," the man reintroduced himself. "And may I tell you, my dear, it's a pleasure to be back."

PART TWO

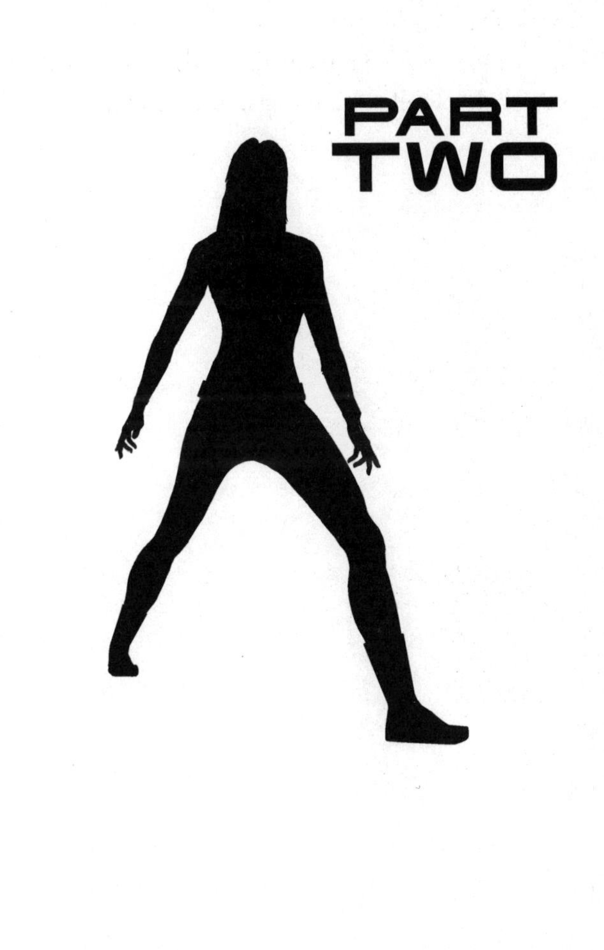

CHAPTER TEN

It was called the Moriarty Syndrome. They'd studied it last term in spycraft. The idea was that perhaps some villains could never be entirely defeated, that some bad guys were indeed so bad, so black, so irredeemably loathsome, that they virtually came to represent evil itself. And just as everyone knew there would always, sadly, be evil in the world, so it seemed likely that some villains could never truly die.

And a case in point, Ben considered, as he struggled violently against the straps of his recliner, was Dr. Averill Frankenstein — insane geneticist and worst customer imaginable for manicurists everywhere. They'd last seen him in the gene chamber of his lodge in the Wildscape. More relevantly for the application of the Moriarty Syndrome, they'd last seen him pretty much dismembered, and with his intestines trailing like links of purple sausages across the lab floor. In short, they'd last seen him pretty much dead.

Yet here was the heir of the Frankensteins alive again, grinning over a captive Bond Team and twining his maggot fingers once more. There was no sign of any of the doctor's trademark genetic mutations, which was only to be welcomed, but that relief was balanced by the shocking presence of one of his companions.

Ben wondered if there was an equivalent Moriarty Syndrome for a fallen teammate who also seemed to have returned from the dead.

Jennifer Chen, by rights, should have been tied up with the

good guys — with those who'd been her friends, with Bex, with Grant. Instead, she was standing with the opposition: Frankenstein, Dr. Scarletti, and a liberal sprinkling of armed guards. And she didn't seem uncomfortable. She regarded the prisoners with cold, emotionless eyes. Jake's groan as he stumbled back toward consciousness found silent echo in Ben's own soul.

And why had Frankenstein brought them here, to the Facial Remolding Center? Why were the seven of them strapped to the recliners, Ben gulped, as if waiting for surgery? He filed *that* thought under "don't go there" and tried to access "team leader morale boosters" instead. There was one grain of comfort: they'd beaten Frankenstein before — they could do it again. He hoped.

"Ah, good, good," Frankenstein was approving as Jake opened his eyes, "now that you can all hear me perhaps we'd better start, though before we do, I would just like to say how wonderful it is to see you all again and looking so well." Frankenstein paused to giggle. "A state of affairs that you probably realize is unlikely to last much longer."

"You're not doing a lot for my health right now, if you really want to know," moaned Eddie.

"What have you done with Sam and the others?" Cally demanded.

"Oh, they're being disposed of elsewhere," Frankenstein said dismissively. "I'm not interested in *them*. Only you. And this charming young lady I've not had the pleasure of meeting before." He hovered over Bex like a vulture.

"Undo the straps, and we can shake hands," Bex suggested sweetly.

"I don't think so, my dear," Frankenstein giggled. "I prefer to keep my hands to myself. I do know who you are, though. Jonathan Deveraux's daughter. A worthy addition to the team, I'm sure."

Lori saw anxiety on Grant's face. "It's all right, sir. We know who Bex is. She told us."

"Of course," Frankenstein picked up on Lori's words. "Between teammates there should be no secrets. So I assume young Rebecca has also told you the truth about her redoubtable father, why he never leaves his room?"

"What?" Ben frowned. "What do you mean, the truth?"

Bex and Grant both shouted, "No!" at the same time, much to Frankenstein's amusement.

"So she hasn't told you? And neither has your senior tutor. Well, I must say I was surprised when I found out, but to keep it a secret from your teammates, your students." A mock sigh. "You just don't know who to trust these days, do you?"

"Well, I don't trust you for a start, Frankenstein!" What was this about Deveraux and the truth? Was Bex still keeping something from them? But it didn't, it couldn't be allowed to matter now. Time for revelations later, if there was a later. Frankenstein was attempting to weaken them by sowing the seeds of suspicion. Bond Team couldn't allow that to work. They had to go on the offensive — as far as you could when strapped helplessly to a recliner and surrounded by guards with guns. "Frankenstein!" Ben scoffed the name. "I don't think so. The real Frankenstein's rotted away to dirt by now. You're just a second-rate pretender. Same for the Grant you planted at Spy High to discredit us. Same for the Jennifer Chen look-alike over there. You're a sick joke. A cheap shot. We're not impressed."

"Ah, but you ought to be, young Ben." Frankenstein loomed

above him like a grotesque scarecrow. "Because, in a very real sense, I *am* Averill Frankenstein. I know it because I remember my death."

"Good times," said Cally.

"I remember my children falling upon me, the children you turned against me —" he pointed accusingly at Cally and Jake — "and I remember them pulling at me and clawing at me and my bones popping out of their sockets and my skin splitting open . . ."

"Dr. Frankenstein," intruded Dr. Scarletti, "are you —?"

"Of course I am, Scarletti." Frankenstein's fingers fluttered waxenly. "So I died. But even death can be put right these days, my young friends. Some of my loyal technicians returned to the ruin of my lodge and discovered my remains, a limb here, an organ there, and they took me away to another lab of mine and commenced a program that, with the foresight of the Frankensteins, I had set up precisely for the unfortunate eventuality of my demise. A cloning program. My knowledge and memories I had already stored in artificial brains, you see, so that my own brand of genius should never be prey to the ravages of mortality. I only needed to be grown another body to make Lazarus look like an amateur, an operation which has been carried out rather successfully, if I may say so." Frankenstein posed like a model at a freak show. "As distinctive as the original."

"You can say that again," Lori commented with distaste.

"But what did Frankenstein do then, I hear you ask."

"Yes. Yes," Eddie said woodenly. "Tell us. What did Frankenstein do then?"

Yes, tell us, Ben urged silently. *Keep talking, you sick lunatic. Give us time to think our way out of this mess. Give us a chance.*

"Well, *then,*" said the doctor, "Frankenstein planned. He planned with two ends in mind. First, there was revenge to be plotted against those responsible for the temporary inconvenience of death: your good selves, of course. Second, there was a world to dominate. I decided to abandon any further experimentation with genetic mutation. Once bitten, twice shy as you might say." A giggle at his own wit. "But to begin with, I wondered if the cloning procedure that had blessed the earth with my return might not also be the answer in other ways. What if I could clone world leaders, generals, opinion formers, the men with their fingers on the buttons, those with the power to mold the minds of the masses? What if I could replace them and render them all subservient to me? An attractive proposition, no?"

"You want an answer to that, scumbag?" snorted Jake.

"So I devoted much of my not inconsiderable ingenuity to the perfection of my cloning technique."

"What are you after, Frankenstein?" Eddie jeered. "The Nobel Prize for megalomania?"

"Meanwhile," the doctor continued unperturbed, "through my secret contacts in the higher echelons of the American government — a most helpful collection of men and women, I have always found — I learned of a certain school operated covertly by a certain father of somebody here and of the certain kind of students that it trained. I learned that some of them had recently been involved in an unexpected action against a mad scientist's wicked operation somewhere in the Wildscape. Apparently, they thwarted his master plan. Apparently, they were heroes. And are we still feeling like heroes now, hmmm? Let me know when you want to start whimpering or begging for mercy. I'll tape it to listen to whenever I'm depressed."

"If we beg, will you shut up?" Eddie wanted to know.

"Ah, that sparky spirit in the face of adversity," Frankenstein sighed. "Enjoy it while you still have lips, Mr. Nelligan. But no, I followed your career with interest after that. I felt close to you, you see. I applauded when you defeated CHAOS, even after my own slight dalliance with the group. I admired when you destroyed Nemesis. And I reached for my Kleenex when I heard of the tragic end of Jennifer here. I nearly came to the funeral, only I worried you might mistake my intentions."

"You piece of filth!" Jake strained at his bonds, enraged. "You're not even fit to say Jennifer's name!"

"Oh, I think I am," Frankenstein corrected, "after all I've done for her lately. What did *you* do, Jake? Oh, that's right. You let her die, didn't you? Myself, I only restored her to life." The white fingers quivered with excitement.

"That's impossible!" Jake looked at Jennifer, so cold, so distant. He refused to believe.

"I dug her up, Jake. Not personally, of course, my hands are far too delicate for manual work." Frankenstein giggled. He was in fine humor. "She'd not been gone long, so I managed to salvage her brain in its entirety, then I borrowed a little bit of her old body — not much, and I won't tell you where from — and I used it to give birth to a new one. Jennifer is a clone, and she belongs to me."

"No!" Jake railed.

"Oh, yes. Who taught you everything you know, my dear?" To Jennifer.

"You did," she said. "Father."

Frankenstein extended his right hand. "Show me your appreciation."

Jennifer took the white dough of his hand between her own. She kissed it. She pressed her cheek against it.

Her eyes, Lori saw, were hollow, vacant. They were like glass.

"No!" Jake again. "You're lying. Jen would never —"

"Never what?" Frankenstein asked. "This is a Jennifer whose mind I have programmed, young Daly, whose brain I have shaped like plastic. She is my child, obedient to none but me. Of you and your little friends, she remembers only what I have taught her to remember. Put simply, Jennifer hates you. With every fiber of her resurrected being."

"No." Jake shook his head vigorously. "I don't believe you."

"I doubted that you would." Frankenstein stepped back and gestured to a guard at a control panel. "Time for our demonstration, I think."

The guard threw a switch, and the straps restraining Jake retracted. He jumped to his feet. Ben noted which control governed their bonds. If one of them could get to it . . . The obvious and only choice for now was "Jake! Free us!"

But Jake wasn't moving, toward the control panel or anywhere else. The world had shrunk again. It was him and Jennifer once more.

But was it her? Or just a clone? "Jennifer? Jen?" That face, that form. Jake fought to keep control of himself. It *was* her. Every detail, every cherished inch of her. He could scarcely comprehend it, but it was Jennifer's body before him now, returned to life. "It's me, Jen. It's Jake. Don't you remember me?" If it was Jennifer, he'd be able to get through to her. He'd be able to reach her. Whatever Frankenstein had done. "Look at me, Jen. You know me, don't you?"

"I know you." Jennifer's smile was like a rictus of death, a movement of muscles only, without warmth. "Jake. I hate you." Like a statement of irrefutable fact.

"No! You don't mean it. You can't mean it, Jen." She was so close to him again, after long, agonizing months of wanting to hold her. "That's him talking, not you. That's Frankenstein."

He scarcely saw the blow coming, but he felt it. Tasted blood in his mouth. Jennifer was in a defensive posture, her reflexes as sharp as in her first life. Jake was staggered, but he did not stop. He heard Frankenstein's giggle, and Ben shouting for him to do something, and Lori's voice, too, sounding like she was frightened. "You don't hate me, Jennifer. You can't!" He rejected everything but her. Fixed his gaze on her. Tried to force the real Jennifer to appear. She *had* to be there.

A second attack battered his ribs. A karate chop sent sickening pains shooting through his neck. Jake buckled, but his eyes did not waver. He held her in them. "I'm Jake, Jen. I love you. Remember? I love you."

It was a kick this time. He did not attempt to block, did not resist. It sent him to his knees, but his gaze remained firm. "Jennifer. Come back. Listen to what I'm saying and come back. We can be together again. Trust me."

"Oh, he's a keeper, I'll give him that," Frankenstein was admiring.

But as Jennifer seized a handful of Jake's black hair and yanked back his head, there seemed to be the glimmer of a response in her own eyes at last. Was it a green spark of recognition, even as she clenched her other hand into a fist and drew it back with deadly intent? Could Jake see her, captive in the clone, caged but struggling to be free?

More time. He was reaching her, he knew it. More time was all he needed.

But Jennifer was screaming with indignant fury. Her fist was quivering with the desire to hurt. There was no more t —

"Wait!" Frankenstein's voice froze Jennifer like ice. "No need to damage him yet, my dear. I think we've proved our point, don't you?" Guards returned Jake to the recliner and refastened the straps. "The old Jennifer is gone forever, I am afraid. The new Jennifer belongs to me."

But even though Frankenstein was stroking her hair with those disgusting fingers like she was his pet or something, Jake realized her eyes were still on him. And was that a line of doubt on her brow?

"You'll be distressed to hear, however," the doctor sighed as he continued, "that my cloning experiments were not in the end as successful as I had hoped."

"Shame," Eddie commiserated.

"You okay, Jake?" Lori whispered across.

"I might be getting there," Jake muttered cryptically.

"Yes," Frankenstein droned, "unfortunately, the clones proved too unreliable too often. Sometimes they lacked the physical stability for prolonged life. They demonstrated a rather nasty tendency to melt without warning: So tiresome to have to clean them up, they leave such terrible stains. And then, other times, it was their minds that limited their effectiveness. The mind of a clone is a complicated business, you understand. Its memories, any memories of its previous life, can be so dangerous. They challenge the clone's sense of self, you see, its individuality. They can make it neurotic, violent, even suicidal."

"Well, if you feel like you're up for a little bit of self-harm, Frankenstein," offered Ben, "don't let us stop you."

"How kind. No, of all the clones I have created, only Jennifer here has endured. And myself, of course. Perhaps we share a stronger survival instinct than our brethren. Perhaps, we have more to live for. What do you think, my dear?" Jennifer did not respond. "In any case, with one further exception, I have destroyed my other clones."

"The exception being mine," deduced Grant.

"Correct. My little joke — to replace the senior tutor of Deveraux Academy with a creation of my own. Useful to isolate the six of you, my young friends, to draw you here, to place you like puppets in my power. But of course —" Frankenstein shrugged — "you only have Mr. Grant himself to blame. If he had not sought the services of Changing Faces, then we would not have been able to take the tissue sample necessary for cloning. My revenge might have been delayed. You might have lived longer. Ah, well, vanity makes victims of us all. Might I just add that it's been a pleasure entertaining you here as our guest, Mr. Grant — all that wonderful information we've pumped out of your brain. But I do feel that the well, as they say, has run dry, so I think it probably best that you set a final good example and expire with your students. And now, I think I've said enough."

"That," observed Eddie, "I find hard to believe."

"Yes, Frankenstein," Ben hurried, desperate for the doctor not to stop. "What's the deal with Changing Faces? I can't believe you're really in it to make people feel better about themselves."

"Ah, Ben," nodded Frankenstein, "you know me so well. And you are, of course, so right. Some clients receive normal treatments, of course, to establish our clinics' credentials, but others, oh, to certain lucky others, we add a little bonus, at no extra charge."

"I'm sure they're thrilled," Eddie murmured.

"Brain implants. Nothing to cause the subject any immediate harm. Just a tiny computer chip snuggled comfortably between the frontal lobes. You could carry it in your head with you for the rest of your life quite safely. Unless of course, it's activated —" Frankenstein sighed self-critically like someone at a support group confessing a minor sin — "and I just can't help activating them. It's simply fun to watch the subject's reaction. The implants augment the fear centers of the brain, you see. They make people insanely paranoid. They turn the mildest-mannered subjects into raging lunatics. At the merest flip of a switch."

"And that's your idea of fun, is it?" despised Cally. "What did you do as a boy, Frankenstein, hang puppies from the backs of chairs?"

"Not quite, my dear, though I did like to see how they worked." Frankenstein's yeasty fingers flexed as if remembering the feel of a puppy between them. "But to the point, as time is pressing. My original plan was to unleash an endless wave of paranoid maniacs across the country before making one or two modest financial demands — you might have seen the occasional trial run on the news — but then a much better idea occurred to me. You see, Changing Faces had just gained an unexpected but important new client."

"The president," gasped Cally.

"Himself," Frankenstein indicated to Dr. Scarletti. "Run the film, Doctor, would you?" On screens around the room, *Procedure*

341: Brain Implant flickered again into life. "It did come as something of a surprise to me," Frankenstein admitted, "but President Westwood does have a brain, after all, as you can see." The camera pulled back, enabling the audience to view the face as well as the exposed brain of the patient. If it wasn't President Graveney Westwood, the most powerful man in the world, then it was his clone. "He came in for a little bit of a complexion refresher," said Frankenstein. "And went away a little bit heavier in the gray matter department. And I do believe I have an appointment with him very soon." He consulted his watch. "Yes, indeed. I'm something of a special adviser to the president now, you know. A trusted confidant. In fact, I'll be accompanying him to the Guardian Star tonight. It's so exciting. I've never been to space before, and it'll certainly be a lot safer than remaining on Earth."

"What are you talking about, Frankenstein?" Ben had one or two ideas. None of them were good.

"Don't worry your handsome blond head about it, Ben," Frankenstein advised. "Believe me, you have more immediate concerns." He snapped his fingers. The clusters of scalpels and blades suspended above each recliner began to whir, began to whirl, like the rotor of a helicopter. Frankenstein giggled as he saw realization dawn in seven sets of eyes. "Dr. Scarletti, explain the purpose of these sharp and shiny slicers for our reluctant guests, will you?"

"Of course, Dr. Frankenstein," Scarletti obliged. "They are skin cutters. When employed by an expert facial remolding surgeon, they can be set to skim off damaged or aging skin from the face of a patient before new layers of fresher and more flattering flesh are applied. The procedure is, of course, carried out under general anesthesia."

"Sadly," apologized Frankenstein, "we seem to be a little short of anesthesia at the moment, but I still think you'll benefit from the treatment. A pity I can't stay and watch, but it's not wise to keep the president waiting. Who knows what he'll do?"

"You're mad, Frankenstein," Grant struggled. "If you think you're going to get away with this —"

"Ah, those old clichés still sound so wonderful, don't they? And my dear Grant, I *am* getting away with it. So farewell, my young friends, for the final time. I'm leaving Dr. Scarletti, the lovely Jennifer, and one or two of my men with you. I wouldn't want your last moments to be lonely ones." The long fingers waved. "And when I say it's been a pleasure, I really do mean it."

The cutter mechanisms clicked. Very slightly, very slowly, the blades began to descend.

"No sweat," Eddie boasted, though the patches under his arms told a different story. "We've been in worse positions than this and still . . . actually, no, we haven't . . ."

"So, Frankenstein," Ben yelled, also trying for the defiance in the face of death approach, "you expect us to beg?"

"No, Ben," giggled Frankenstein. "I expect you to scream."

Metal clamps sprang from the tops of the recliners and seized the captives' heads. There was going to be no looking away.

The sleek, circling scalpels dipped ever closer.

"Frankenstein!" Eddie cried suddenly. "What about Operation Grand Slam?"

"What?" The doctor paused in the doorway. "What are you talking about?"

"Don't worry," Eddie groaned. "It was worth a try. Worked for the other guy."

And Frankenstein was gone, leaving only his customary high-pitched giggle behind him.

"So what now?" There was an edge of panic in Lori's voice. "Ben, what do we do?"

The skin cutters sliced toward them. Their sound was like a swarm of insects.

"What do we do?" Despairingly, Ben saw his death barely inches away. "I only wish I knew."

CHAPTER ELEVEN

"Jennifer!" Jake could still see her, even though the head clamps restricted his range of vision. She seemed to have edged closer to him now that Frankenstein was gone. "You've got to help us. You're the only one who can. You've got to remember who you are, who *we* are." And quickly, Jake knew, before the scalpels went to work and memories of them would be all that was left.

"You're wasting your time, boy," predicted Dr. Scarletti. "Dr. Frankenstein's processing is infallible."

Better not be. Jake felt a caressing breeze on his cheek and brow as the blades whirled closer.

"Jen, we need you!"

And she was wincing like she had a sudden headache, her lips struggling to form forbidden words. She was beside him now.

"Say her name!" Jake shouted for the others' benefit.

A barrage of "Jennifers" bombarded her eardrums, clearly distressing her. She cried out and thrust her hands over her ears, staggering toward Jake's recliner as if she was about to fall.

Maybe Dr. Scarletti's faith in Frankenstein was only superficial, after all. "Some assistance here!" she called to a guard, approached Jennifer with the haste of concern, held her shoulders.

Jennifer's lashing elbow took her down. A kick did the same for the guard. Frankenstein's men had been briefed to take no chances. They opened fire. Dr. Scarletti's final usefulness in life was as a shield for Jennifer.

"Hurry, Jen!" Jake screamed.

She raced from behind Scarletti's body like quicksilver, darting beneath the gunfire, striking out with foot and fist to gain the control panel, to flip the release switch.

Her former teammates could move sharply, too, particularly when the alternative was a little impromptu facial remolding. The guards had swung around to aim at Jennifer. They were slow to recognize that the threat was now on two fronts. They weren't conscious long enough to dwell on it.

Only Jake did not vent his anger on Frankenstein's men. He rushed directly to Jennifer, embraced her, clasped her close in dizzy disbelief. "Jen!" She was warm. She was alive. She was restored to him.

"Jake?" Her real voice, not cold now, no sound of Frankenstein left in it. "I don't understand. Where are we? What happened to me?"

"It's all right. It doesn't matter." He kissed her, soothed her. "You're back with me now. You're safe."

Lori watched Jake and Jennifer. Ben watched Lori. Was that disappointment he detected, there in Lori's expression? Jake wouldn't need a substitute for Jennifer now, even if a willing volunteer had been available. Ben waited for his girlfriend to turn to him. He waited quite awhile.

"Saved by the skin of our teeth," Bex said, slipping her hand into Eddie's.

"Saved by the skin of our everything," Eddie replied. The scalpels were busily slashing the leather of the recliners to ribbons. "That could have been us."

"Could-have-beens don't leave scars," said Cally, "but I think I'll turn them off, anyway. I'll feel better."

"Yeah?" said Ben. "Well, I'll feel better when somebody

actually starts to mean what she says." He stabbed his finger at Bex. "What was all this no-more-secrets stuff back at Spy High, Ms. Deveraux? How come we have to find out from Frankenstein that there's still something you haven't told us?"

"Ben, I didn't —"

Grant intervened. "Bex was not at liberty to reveal highly classified information, Ben, not even under such extreme circumstances as those you've had to deal with. She was wrong to tell you her true identity in the first place —" he ran his hands through his hair — "though disciplinary procedures may have to wait awhile."

"But I think we deserve to know, sir," Ben pressed. "If Bex is on our team, surely we have a right. Why *is* Mr. Deveraux never seen in public?"

"Leave it, Ben." The finality of Grant's tone was absolute. "We have more important priorities right now." He retrieved a weapon from a fallen guard. "We have to get back to the academy as quickly as possible. There's still Frankenstein's scheme to thwart, and I for one am looking forward to having a quiet little word with whoever's sitting behind my desk."

Ben had to concede that the senior tutor was right. For now, at least. But this was one matter that he wasn't going to let rest.

"Why is Ben so angry?" Jennifer clung to Jake like she was afraid of the world.

"Stanton's always uptight," Jake said. "He was born that way. Don't you remember?"

"I think so." He could see her almost trying to wring the past from her mind like drops of precious water from a sponge. "But that girl with green hair, I don't . . . Should I know her? I can't . . ."

"No, don't worry. That's Bex," Jake comforted. "She's new. She's your —" He stopped himself just in time.

"My what?" Had he been in time? He didn't want to say replacement because that raised the question of why Jennifer had needed to be replaced. Jake doubted it was wise to go there. "My what, Jake?"

"Nothing. It doesn't matter, Jen. Come on, we've got to go."

"But it does matter. It all matters." She squeezed her eyes shut. "Why am I so confused about everything? If only I could *remember* . . ."

Jake found himself praying she wouldn't.

Ben had hoped for a flight back to Spy High on one of Deveraux's private jets — returning from the skies on wings of glory kind of thing. But Grant suggested that his clone might have had them shot down en route. Deveraux jets, while the quickest available means of travel, were also the most conspicuous. The senior tutor would sooner sacrifice a few hours of time than their lives, a position with which even Ben found it difficult to disagree. His triumphant vindication would have to wait. The anonymity of public transport it was.

At least they were traveling first class, and the Eastliner Light Train was making swift progress. Grant was in the communications car trying to contact the school. Everybody else was in the train's luxurious lounge car and grouped around a perplexed Jennifer Chen, who was gripping Jake's hand tightly and glancing nervously between her former teammates.

"Just hope this journey's not going to be as eventful as the *last* time we let the train take the strain," observed Cally.

"Absolutely." Ben peered at Jennifer like a doctor at a

patient. He recalled Nemesis sabotaging the Light Train from the domes. "Do you remember that, Jen?"

A blank, troubled expression implied that she didn't.

"So what *do* you remember, Jen?" Cally probed, as coaxingly as possible. "You know who we all are, don't you?"

"Yes, of course." Not that she sounded too confident. "Except for Bex, and Jake's told me who she is."

"Yep," Bex grinned. "Once seen, never forgotten, that's me." Though with the others transfixed by the reappearance of Jennifer, she felt she was maybe overstating the case. She could probably pick all their pockets right now, and they wouldn't notice.

"And I remember Spy High, of course." Jennifer concentrated like a child in a spelling bee. "That's our school, isn't it? I can remember being there. The rooms are like pictures in my head but like old pictures and they're faded, kind of worn. And they're jumbled up like someone's emptied a photo album on the floor, and I want to put them in the right order again but I can't." She appealed to her friends for help. "I can't do it."

Cally and Lori took her other hand. It was trembling. It was cold. "You mustn't worry, Jen," Lori said. "We'll get you back to school. The docs'll take a look at you. You'll be fine. Promise."

"You just need some rest is all," Cally added. "Trust us."

"But where were we? Before, I mean. And why was I there?" Rather than relaxing, Jennifer seemed to be growing more agitated. "Was I captured or something? Brainwashed? Turned against you? I was, wasn't I?"

"Jen," Jake soothed, "all that's over. You came through when it mattered, and you're back with us again."

"I was brainwashed. You don't need to tell me. I can remember . . . something about a room. I was in a room, a room with no windows. . . . And I remember someone in there with me and his voice in my ear and in my head, filling my mind, and . . . and . . ." She was groping for her past as for signposts in the fog.

Ben saw the concern in Jake's eyes. He shared it. What had Frankenstein said? The memory of a clone was a dangerous thing. There'd been no reason for him to lie about that. "Listen, Jennifer," he said, "and I'm speaking as team leader now. Don't try to remember anything. You'll only get yourself stressed, and, like Cally said, you need rest, recovery time. We'll be at Spy High soon, and we can take things from there, but for now Jake's right — we're all just glad you're back. Bond Team hasn't been the same without you."

Ben felt Lori's approving smile on him. He also saw, out of the corner of his eye, Bex Deveraux doing a fine job of disguising her own worries with a display of teeth. Ben could guess what she was anxious about. A Spy High team numbered six, not seven. Jen might soon be wanting her old bed back.

"Think I'll go see if Mr. Grant's reached anyone at the school yet," Bex said. Nobody seemed to notice. And when she got up to leave and when she did leave, nobody seemed to notice that, either.

The call had both surprised and delighted the man who sat at Senior Tutor Elmore Grant's desk, the man who wore Senior Tutor Elmore Grant's face. The surprise had resulted both from the identity of the caller — he'd thought Dr. Frankenstein would already be in space by now — and the nature of the doctor's news: That somehow Bond Team had escaped elimination once again and were very likely heading for home. The delight arose because the teenagers' good fortune, which was not to last, provided the clone with the opportunity to prove his worth to his creator once and for all.

He activated the desk communicator. "Corporal Keene to Senior Tutor Grant's study at once." He'd have the resilient whelps dealt with, let Frankenstein see if he didn't. He felt like a good son wanting to make his father proud.

His mood was spoiled a little, however, when he switched off the communicator. His finger clung to the device like gum, had to be peeled away like sticking plaster, leaving a milky smear of skin behind. The clone frowned. Maybe he should have used voice control. But what did it matter? With any luck, his work here was nearly complete, and if he now had to flannel his fingers with his handkerchief as well as mop his brow, then it was probably just that the air-conditioning wasn't working with the necessary efficiency. Anyway, he didn't have time to think about it. With his usual military punctuality, here was Keene.

"Sir, you wanted to see me?"

"Indeed I did, Keene." The clone was brisk, businesslike. "The renegades — Bond Team — I have received intelligence that they have eluded the grad team and are still at liberty. My sources tell me that they are on their way back here, no doubt to try again to plead their innocence."

Keene's lips were set in such a straight line that it was remarkable any coherent language could be formed. "May I ask what sources, sir?"

"You may not. What you may do is prepare to take charge of our final and decisive action against these dangerous traitors."

"And what might that be, sir?" Though the corporal's eyes suggested he already knew.

"Isn't it obvious? As soon as they show themselves, we remove their threat. Permanently. Something we should have done in the first place."

"Sir," cautioned Keene, observing his superior closely, remembering what Stanton had said in the SkyBike hangar, "before we take such a drastic step, I feel we need to appraise Mr. Deveraux himself of the situation."

"What you feel is not a matter of concern, Corporal." It must have been growing warmer. The senior tutor's already sopping handkerchief was out soaking up the sweat from his hands. "Mr. Deveraux will be informed in due course. For now, I will personally take responsibility for what must be done."

"In that case, sir," Keene said staunchly, "I would like my objection noted to what I consider to be a premature and disproportionate response of —"

"Objection so noted, Keene," the clone said, not even attempting to disguise the contempt in his voice. "And as I wouldn't want to offend your newfound sensitivities, perhaps I had better remove you entirely from the Bond Team operation and confine you to other duties."

If Keene had been a less disciplined soldier, at that point he might have punched the air and betrayed himself. "Is that an order, sir?"

"If you want to put it like that, Corporal," scorned the clone, "then yes, I suppose it is."

"Thank you, sir," said Keene.

Jennifer was sleeping now, though Jake still sat beside her holding her hand. He gazed at her with a fierce protectiveness, branding her features onto his brain in case he should ever lose her again. But he wouldn't. Not this time. Fate had given the two of them a second chance, and even though Fate was fickle, it'd have to fight its way past him if it ever wanted to mess with Jennifer again.

"Jake, can we talk?" Lori, gnawing her lower lip uncertainly.

"Sure." His attention not straying from Jennifer. "What about?"

"*Who*," Lori said, settling alongside Jake. "Jen."

"Yeah, I know." Somehow, he didn't want to look at Lori. "She's gonna need a lot of medical attention, I know that. And we'll have to be careful how we reintroduce her memories, maybe even which memories, but she's gonna be fine, isn't she, and —"

"Jake," Lori interrupted quietly, firmly, "that's not Jennifer."

"What are you talking about, Lo? Use your eyes. You can see she's Jennifer."

"It's a clone, Jake, a copy. All right, so it —"

"It?" Growled like an animal protecting its mate.

"*She* shares Jennifer's DNA — maybe some or even all of her memories, too. But this body didn't experience those things, Jake. This Jennifer's like an actress taking over a role established by somebody else. She's not our Jennifer. Our Jennifer is . . ."

Now his gaze did snap to Lori, and it was burning, intense. "I know what our Jennifer is, Lo. You don't need to tell me. I *know* she's dead. I held her in my arms, and I held her hand like I'm doing now, and then her skin was cold like ice, and now it's warm again, alive again. So what are you saying, Lo? I shouldn't be grateful? I shouldn't love her anymore? I should wish her back beneath the ground?"

"No, no, no," Lori winced painfully. "But be careful, Jake. Maybe . . . try not to get too involved. If something happens, I mean . . ."

"Nothing will," Jake stated. "I won't let it."

Farther down the lounge, Cally sighed. "I don't think she's getting through to him."

"I didn't think she would." Ben stared out of the window as the landscape flashed by. "But it was Lori's idea to try."

Cally defended her friend from the implied criticism. "So what's your idea, Ben?"

"I don't think I have one right now. The sooner we get back to Spy High and clear our names, the better. Then we can go after Frankenstein, and then Jennifer Version 2 can be tested and treated by specialists who know what they're doing. I mean, should she even be *told* she's a clone? Told she died? What would the effect of that be? I just don't know, Cally."

"And there was me thinking you had an answer for everything," Cally said, not unkindly.

"Yeah, well, I don't. Sorry."

"You don't have to be sorry, Ben." Cally looked toward the sleeping Jennifer. "Let's just hope Grant can contact Jonathan Deveraux before anything else can go wrong."

Sadly for Cally, the chances of the senior tutor contacting anyone at Spy High at the moment were not looking good. Right now, the communications car seemed to be something of a misnomer. "All the usual channels seem to be out of action." Grant frowned, drumming his fingers on the console. "Even my direct line to your father."

Bex, sitting alongside him, spread her hands sympathetically. "I don't know," she sighed. "You leave for five minutes, and the whole place goes to pot."

"Particularly when my clone is no doubt having the time of his artificial life sabotaging the academy's communications and every other system as well," glowered Grant. He ran his hands through his hair as if to remind himself that he was the human Elmore Grant. "Well, the day I let myself be outwitted by a pale imitation is the day I retire. He wouldn't need my brain to guess I'd try to get in touch with your father. But there's someone else I know we can trust, one last course we can try."

"And if that doesn't work, either?" Bex ventured.

"Then," Grant said grimly, "we're in trouble."

IGC DATA FILE GRT 3817

. . . final press conference before departing to a classified location for his space shuttle flight to the Guardian Star. The president drew applause and laughter in equal measure from the assembled media as he answered questions in his space suit. "I wanted to wear the helmet, too," he revealed. "But Dick [Press Secretary Dick Chambers] wouldn't let me. Said what's a good photo opportunity if the people can't see your face?"

Once again, President Westwood praised the work of the scientists and technicians who made EPI in general and the Guardian Star in particular a reality. "Thanks to those brilliant men and women," he said, "decent Americans can sleep safely in their beds at night, while the enemies among us had better look to the skies and tremble. Their day is done."

President Westwood singled out for special mention his advisory team headed by Dr. Victor Averill. "These are people who are not household names, but they ought to be," he declared. "I have a feeling that maybe my little trip to the Guardian Star is going to change all that."

The president's high spirits extended to the final question of the session: What did it feel like to be on the brink of becoming America's first president in space? "Memorable," President Westwood acknowledged. "Truly memorable. I think I can guarantee that this will be a moment none of us are likely to forget. . . ."

It would only be a matter of time. Soon the wretched Bond Team would show themselves, and he would have them, their annoying heads on a platter — preferably literally. The clone leaned back in his chair at the senior tutor's desk and anticipated his victory. He wondered if the original Grant had kept a bottle of the hard stuff in his study somewhere for celebratory purposes. He supposed he ought to remember. Perhaps in one of these cabinets over here. No such luck. Pity. But was that a shock blaster he could see . . . ?

The study door burst open with the impudence of someone laughing during prayers.

"Corporal Keene." The false Grant drew himself erect. "What do you think you're doing? How dare you barge into the senior tutor's study like this?"

"Senior tutor?" Keene made the sound of a barking dog that for him approximated to amusement. "What senior tutor?"

He knew. Somehow, Keene knew. The clone hadn't been programmed to panic, but he did anyway, made a grab for the shock blaster in the cabinet.

"I wouldn't touch that if I were you," came a second uncomfortably familiar voice, "or even if you were me." The Senior Tutor Elmore Grant who now entered the study was already holding a shock blaster, and it wasn't pointing at Keene.

"It can't be," breathed the clone, backing away instinctively. "No . . ."

"I'm afraid that's a yes," corrected Grant. "We meet again. First my home, now my study. I think I can see a pattern emerging."

"And believe us, this is only the start of your problems." Ben led Bond Team into the study, too. The clone gaped.

"Mr. Grant!" greeted Eddie. "Hi! Did you miss us?"

"Faked any film lately?" Jake wanted to know.

"But how did you . . . ?" The clone struggled to understand. The sweat dribbled thickly down his face.

"Get in here without being spotted?" Lori thoughtfully completed his sentence. "Oh, we had a little help."

"You'd be surprised how interested Corporal Keene was to hear from us," Bex added. "Came right out to the station to meet us, he did, *and* shielded us from security. Such a nice man, not like some I could mention."

"What's the matter, Mr. Grant?" jeered Cally. "Things getting a little hot for you?"

It seemed so. The clone was surrounded now, hemmed in. And the perspiration was pouring from him, his shirt, trousers, even his jacket was sticking wetly to his body as if he'd walked fully clothed into a sauna. "No," he said. "No." And he opened his fists and his hands were like melting wax, the fingers drooping and lolling as if they'd suddenly been filleted. He showed them to Grant, Keene, and the students, a wail of horror rising in his throat. "Help me. Help me!"

"We can't," said Grant, which sounded a little less harsh than "we won't," though perhaps also less honest.

The clone might have said more, only at that point his upper lip began to ooze over the lower one. Indeed, his entire head seemed now to be liquefying, like ice cream left out in the sun. He swayed unsteadily on his feet as his legs leaked out from his trouser bottoms.

"Oh, gross," Eddie grimaced, looking like a bout of regurgitation might be in order. "Anybody got a bucket?"

"For you?" said Bex.

"No way. For him."

"Don't look, Jen." Jake held her protectively as fear clutched him in turn. The clones were unstable, Frankenstein had told them that, but only now could they see what "unstable" meant. The Grant clone, maybe due to the stress of discovery, was de-solidifying at an alarming rate, flesh turned to fluid spilling from his sleeves. But Jennifer was a clone, too. Was this grisly fate also destined to be hers? It couldn't be.

"Get back!" warned Grant.

With a wet plop, his former clone imploded, his body now no more than a viscous, gelatinous substance that popped and bubbled like milky lava on the carpet, his clothes lying incongruously in its midst.

"Yeesh," said Eddie. "The cleaner's gonna love us."

"All right." Restored to his rightful position, Grant took charge. "The clone was a distraction, nothing more. The real danger is Frankenstein, and we may still be in time to stop the president's shuttle from liftoff."

"Sounds good, sir," said Ben, "but how?"

"Ben, all of you, I think perhaps it's finally time for you to meet Mr. Deveraux."

CHAPTER TWELVE

Under other circumstances, Ben would have been glorying in it. He was the first Spy High student in history, along with the other members of Bond Team — and Bex, of course, who didn't really count — to come face to face with Mr. Jonathan Deveraux himself, to look him directly in the eye rather than through the medium of a videoscreen. This had been major among Ben's ambitions since the day he joined the school, and now it was happening. It was just so annoying that the threat of Frankenstein was spoiling it somewhat, rushing it, subordinating it to weightier matters of world security. Which was one more reason to pay the good doctor back.

Grant led them into Deveraux's rooms on the floor where Lori had lost Bex several nights before, only the rooms here turned out to be a circular elevator that probed its passengers with light.

"Complete physical analysis down to DNA level in less than five seconds," said Grant. "Mr. Deveraux is very choosy about who gets in to see him."

"Can we do the light thing again?" Eddie requested. "It kind of tickled."

Grant ignored him. "I'd ask you to prepare yourselves for what you're about to see." *Not who?* Cally wondered. "Mr. Deveraux is not what you might be expecting."

The curved elevator door whisked open. For a moment, Ben thought it must have taken them down, to the core of Spy High, rather than up, to the founder's top floor accommodation. There were no living quarters here, no furniture or carpeting or paintings on the wall. Instead, their surroundings were more like the IGC, with computers paneling the glistening metal perimeter, and a great ring of screens suspended from the ceiling, leaning inward like gossips, and the mosaic floor pulsing and lighting up to track the movements of the visitors as their weight shifted. Sensors and circuitry bulged from the walls like cybernetic muscles, traceries of wires like delicate veins, and electronic power pumping with the easy regularity of a heartbeat. There seemed to be only one chair in the entire vast room, and that was vacant, raised on a round platform in the center of the screen circle with some kind of black helmet hanging just above it. Of Mr. Jonathan Deveraux, there appeared to be no sign.

Bond Team wandered wonderingly into the center of the room. Bex stayed beside Grant and Keene. Her father's quarters did not come as a surprise to her.

"Very smart," Eddie whistled.

"These machines, this equipment." Cally was like a child at Christmas. "I've never seen anything like it."

But Ben felt cheated. "I thought you were bringing us to Mr. Deveraux, sir."

"I have," said Grant. "Mr. Deveraux is here."

"Where?"

"All around you." He gestured expansively. "Mr. Deveraux is the computer."

Elsewhere, at a military base in the Mojave Desert that appears on no maps and that officially does not exist, the most powerful man in the world was being given his final briefing before boarding the presidential shuttle.

"Conditions are perfect, sir," said an aide. "This bird's so smooth, you won't even know you're flying."

"That's fine." President Graveney Westwood inclined his head. If the aide had peered more closely at his commander in chief's skull, which of course, he didn't, he might just have been able to make out the faintest of scars, the kind of scars left by laser sealants after advanced brain surgery. "I'm sure everything is just fine."

"May I say, sir," ventured the aide, "you're in a mighty relaxed mood for a man about to take his first trip into space."

"Oh, that's because I know I have nothing to worry about," said Westwood. "Isn't that right, Averill?" He turned to the man with the long fingers beside him, the man who bobbed and swiveled on his hips like the two halves of his body were about to part company.

"That's right, Mr. President," the man agreed, with a high-pitched giggle that made the aide think of dark nights and lunatic asylums. "There's nothing for you to worry about at all."

So the Jonathan Deveraux who spoke to them from the Spy High screen wasn't really Jonathan Deveraux at all, not in a flesh-and-blood sense, in any case. Couldn't be. Jonathan Deveraux's actual flesh and blood had been cremated more than ten years ago, reduced to a small pile of ash and preserved somewhere in a jar like salt in a salt cellar. The austerely handsome face that appeared from time to time to instruct or inspire the students, it was the face of a ghost, a memory. Those features that might have been molded from steel, those piercing eyes that glittered with purpose and conviction, were reconstructions, technology. Eddie had once commented that Jonathan

Deveraux looked like God without the beard. In that, the founder had beaten death, would never age now, maybe he wasn't too far away.

And there were more Jonathan Deverauxs than might have been thought. Ben counted three of them now, three giant virtual faces inspecting them from the circle of screens. One was smiling down upon Bex, one was occupied with Grant, while the third was left to consider the rest of Bond Team and Corporal Keene. It gave Ben a not altogether uplifting indication of his rank in the founder's list of priorities.

"My father died when I was very young," Bex was explaining, "but there was no funeral, no obituary, no announcement of death. He'd been ill a long time, one of those illnesses that even now you don't get better from. He knew what was coming. He made plans for it."

"Did you know?" Lori was both horrified and fascinated. "About this?"

Bex shook her head and smiled almost apologetically. "I'd never known my mother, and then I thought I'd lost my father as well."

"You could not have been told at that age, Rebecca," her watching father said. "You would not have understood."

Ben wasn't sure he understood now. Even as one Deveraux was contributing to *their* conversation, the image nearest to Grant seemed to be speaking to *him*. Could the computerized man multiply his existence like that, function in more than one place at a time, subdivide himself yet still retain a unified personality? It was incredible. And what must Bex have felt when first she discovered the truth?

As if in direct response: "On my tenth birthday, I was

brought here, to this school, to this room. They told me I was going to see something wonderful and that I shouldn't be afraid. I did and I wasn't. I saw my father again, and I knew I wasn't alone. While his body was still alive, you see, Dad had had his brain patterns digitized and uploaded onto the most powerful computer that the resources of the ninth richest man in the world could create. Not just his memories and his knowledge, that would have been easy, but his entire personality, his essence, his dreams, his ideals. A religious person might say his soul."

"Software does not have a soul," said Jonathan Deveraux with faint amusement, "but otherwise, my students, what Rebecca has told you is true."

"No wonder he doesn't get out much," muttered Eddie. The revelations had staggered him as much as his teammates. It seemed nobody stayed dead in the spy game. Frankenstein, poor Jennifer, and now even Deveraux himself. The real and the unreal seemed the same. *Feet on the ground, Nelligan,* he urged himself. *Hold on to that sanity. Quip. Joke. Don't take anything seriously. 'Cause if you do, you might well end up in a room with no sharp corners on the furniture and being fed soup through a straw.*

"Mr. Deveraux?" Eddie heard Ben asking. "What's happening with Mr. Grant?"

He saw what Ben meant. Grant was now seated in the chair on the raised platform, and the helmet had been lowered was now attached to his head. The senior tutor was silent, but the triplet of Deverauxs seemed intent on hearing him.

"The cyber-cap allows Mr. Grant to communicate with me telepathically," Bond Team's Deveraux supplied. "Human speech is so laborious. The tongue is like an instrument of lead. And from what Grant is telling me, time is very much of the essence."

The room began to throb with a life of its own. Deveraux was doing something. "I am contacting our agents in the military, in the government. We must locate the president before . . ." He paused thoughtfully. "Before . . ."

"Who'd have guessed a computer'd be so good at building tension?" said Eddie.

"Father?" Bex. "What is it?"

The finely sculptured features of Jonathan Deveraux betrayed no emotion. "We have failed," he said matter-of-factly. "The president is in the air."

Most people in the world had never seen President Graveney Westwood with his mouth hanging open. Lolling jaws had a negative impact on the public perception of their owner, his media advisers had assured him. It tended to suggest stupidity, and, of course, it wouldn't do for the president to be thought of as stupid. Keep your mouth shut, that was the media men's advice, and cultivate the square-jawed expression of imperious command that scores so highly in the approval ratings.

Sadly for President Westwood, none of his media advisers were within earshot right now, not here in the shuttle with the rim of the Earth far below and apparently only deep space ahead. Perhaps they would have forgiven him the slack-jawed look for a moment though, bearing in mind that his present view, the black and icy currents of the void, with its frosted crust of stars, and our own blue and green globe reduced in significance to a ball a child might play with, was so striking and humbling as to reduce anyone to wonder.

But wonder was not the reason for the glaze over the

president's eyes. The man alongside him was. The man who whispered in his ear like the serpent to Eve.

"What you can hear from the passenger compartments, Mr. President," soothed Dr. Averill Frankenstein, "don't let it disturb you." As if the screams and gurgles of dying soldiers would ever trouble the most powerful man in the world. "Just a minor disagreement back there, that's all." A high-pitched giggle. "Men who are loyal to myself — and therefore loyal to you, Mr. President — are removing from our way those who are not. Eliminating our enemies, Mr. President, and you don't like enemies, do you?"

The president didn't. "Enemies . . ." he groped. "All around us . . . anywhere, everywhere . . . we must be eternally vigilant . . ."

"Oh, we will be," approved Frankenstein. "Eternally vigilant. There's a phrase worth a few votes. And that's why we're here, isn't it, Mr. President — to be vigilant."

"Here?" President Westwood was seeing only empty space.

A finger pointing like a long white signpost assisted him. "The Guardian Star, Mr. President. Don't you remember?"

The space station suddenly loomed ahead, a gleaming metal wheel rotating peacefully in the heavens. At its hub, the control center and docking bays, then the spokes, looking fragile and delicate as the light of the sun caught them. These were the corridors leading to the rim of the wheel, pockmarked and punctuated with the rows of missile launchers and gun turrets that comprised the weapons systems of the Guardian Star. Weapons with the potential to decimate the globe, but nothing to worry about, no need to protest — it's all for the earth's protection.

The president smiled when he saw it, like a child rediscovering a favorite toy. "Enemies," he articulated. "They're everywhere . . ."

"How true," acknowledged Dr. Frankenstein, "but never mind." He patted President Westwood on the back (best not to touch the head). "Not for very much longer."

If the situation wasn't so perilous, it would be amusing, Ben thought. Over a year of desperately wanting to meet Mr. Deveraux personally, to be permitted into the holiest of holies of his apartments, and now he was there for the second time in a day. Annoyingly for him, so were the seven other leaders of the current Spy High teams, including, by necessity, the abject Simon Macey. At least Ben wasn't limited to the same kind of wide-eyed astonishment as his peers. Macey was looking like he'd just seen his parents naked or something. At least Ben was still marked out as different from the rest, and that was what he'd always wanted. A Stanton should always stand apart.

They were faced by only a single image of Deveraux at the moment, keeping things simple. ". . . unsustainable and unfair for only one team to know the truth," he was saying. "Therefore, it is appropriate for you all to learn more about my reasons for founding this academy before we may be called into action once again.

"For most of my human life, I was not a good man. Arrogant, self-centered, uncaring of others, I pursued my twin goals of wealth and status without any regard for the consequences. Coldly, callously, ruthlessly." Why was Simon Macey glancing his way and smirking? Ben wondered. "I paid no attention to those I ruined as I grew more powerful, no heed to those whose businesses I destroyed as my empire expanded, no thought to the lives I blighted. Jonathan Deveraux became a name that was revered and despised in equal measure, the name of one of the richest and most influential men in the world. Not that I cared what the ignorant masses thought of me. Presidents courted my company. The most beautiful women fought one another to be seen by my side. In time, I chose one to remain there. My business interests spanned the globe. Whole nations were subservient to me. I possessed everything I wanted, and I wanted to possess everything.

"But a moment comes to any life, perhaps, which places a mirror before it, and reflects a truth which has been hidden and obscured for so many years. My moment came with the birth of my daughter and the death of my wife. An heir to the Deveraux fortune, a carrier of the Deveraux genes, but as I held my only child in my arms, I looked beyond myself for the first time and saw clearly the kind of world she would inherit. A world of greed and selfishness, a world of division and disharmony, the good earth ransacked and raped for profit and pleasure. Poisoned oceans. Stinking skies. A new breed of terrorists and madmen crazed by lust for power ravaging the continents, jeopardizing the survival of the human race itself. And most damning, more unforgivable of all, this was a world that I had unthinkingly and irresponsibly helped to create. The fault was mine, but how could it be rectified?"

The face of Jonathan Deveraux faded as if in defeat, and a second materialized, identical to the first. "Through you, my students, through those who preceded you and those who will follow. Through this institution, Deveraux Academy, dedicated to the training of the next generation of elite secret agents, brave and talented young people willing to risk their lives for the sake of tomorrow."

This second Deveraux sighed and gave way to a third. "But then, as my life began to have new purpose, new meaning, I learned that I was not to have either for long. I was dying. My body could not be saved. And yet, I could not bear to leave my dream for Deveraux Academy incomplete, unfulfilled. I had to survive. I had to find a way. And I did, as you can see. Jonathan Deveraux is dead, yet Jonathan Deveraux lives on."

The face of Deveraux split into two. "And the work of the school continues as it always must, until the threats to our security are no more, until evil men . . ."

". . . like Dr. Frankenstein —" the speech passed from mouth to mouth like a baton in a relay race — "are vanquished for good. I have to tell you, team . . ."

". . . leaders —" as the images doubled again — "that our friends in the military are at this very moment contacting the Guardian Star. The personnel there will be placed on alert, fearing a threat to the president's life. It is to be hoped . . ."

". . . that Frankenstein will be apprehended and the crisis averted . . ."

". . . before it is too late."

Commander of the Guardian Star Ellery Harmon waited nervously by the airlock to Docking Bay One for the president and his party to emerge. He was accompanied by Major Zane Dowling, commanding officer of the small group of Marines aboard the space station, as had always been the plan, and by several armed soldiers as well, which had not. Curse that garbled message from Openshaw earthside. What did he mean, the president was in danger? Who from, up here? Little green men? Harmon was skeptical as to the usefulness of the Guardian Star in defense terms, though absolutely convinced as to its importance with regard to his own career. If only communications hadn't broken up at that point, he might have had a better idea. Of course, he'd got the techs working flat out at reestablishing contact with Earth, preferably before President Westwood wanted to make the inevitable self-congratulatory broadcast to the folks back home. He'd better play it safe and persuade the president to take a preliminary tour of the installation first. This visit could be the making of him if things went well.

Such were the thoughts of a man in his final minute of life.

The airlock light switched from red to green. The airlock door eased open. President Graveney Westwood stepped aboard the Guardian Star, his special adviser Dr. Averill and a small, somehow suspicious clutch of soldiers following.

"Mr. President," Harmon saluted, "I'm Commander Ellery Harmon. It gives me great pleasure to welcome you to the Guardian Star. I sincerely —"

"Why the soldiers, Harmon?" questioned the president. His fellow arrivals were fanning out behind him, only Dr. Averill staying close.

"Ah, sir," Harmon sweated, "a slight security situation seems to have arisen, though I'm sure it's nothing."

"Are you?" said the president. "Oh, dear."

When the firing started, he didn't even flinch.

There was something they weren't telling her. She might be confused about most things just now, but Jennifer Chen still had sense enough to realize that. Why else were her teammates unwilling to meet her gaze or answer her questions? They were behaving like they would with an elderly relative or someone with a terminal disease. Even Jake. He held her, he told her that everything was going to be all right, but in his eyes she could see secrets, she could sense doubt.

Well, if nobody was going to tell her, she'd have to find out for herself.

After their meeting with Jonathan Deveraux, they'd taken her to the infirmary for observation — observation of what? Giving the medics the slip had been easy, and now Jennifer was roaming the corridors of Spy High, trying to make sense of them, trying to use her immediate environment as a catalyst to unlock those doors in her memory that remained stubbornly, frustratingly closed.

It was a strange sensation. Jennifer seemed to know her way around, she remembered the school and that she was a student here, but she had no direct recollection of its geography. She couldn't have described to anyone how to get from A to B, but instinctively she managed herself. And she was becoming more purposeful, too, as if some deep part of her was taking control and leading her toward . . . what?

The plaque on the wall outside read HALL OF HEROES.

Jennifer entered. She knew what was here. Holographic reminders of the Fallen, those who had perished in the cause, fighting evil. It was a sad place but a gentle place, too, a place for reflection.

It was also deserted for now, so nobody heard Jennifer's strangled cry.

One of the holograms. One of the dead. It was her.

One of the dead.

Jennifer staggered backward as the past punched into her brain like a pile driver through a wall, shattering, devastating.

Her body wasn't working. Her body wasn't hers. She felt alien, unknown. She nearly fell among the Fallen.

The truth tore at her mind like talons. Not complete yet, still distant, but advancing, approaching. She could not resist it.

No wonder they didn't want to tell her.

And as Jennifer shook in the Hall of Heroes, the bell suddenly rang through the school like the announcement of catastrophe.

CHAPTER THIRTEEN

The entire student body gathered in the Briefing Room while the bell's ring still echoed.

"Jen." Jake seemed surprised that she was among them. "Shouldn't you be in the infirmary?"

"I was," Jennifer said, sitting beside him. "But I'm not now."

"Are you okay?"

Considering she'd just found her own memorial, she felt surprisingly calm. But she needed to keep that discovery to herself for the moment. Wait until everything was clear. Learn to cope. She was alive now, and life was always precious.

Along the line of seats, she saw Cally and Lori regarding her anxiously, Eddie giving her a thumbs up, Ben nodding cautiously, the new girl, Deveraux's daughter, smiling uncertainly. At least she knew why Bex was there now — the Fallen had to be replaced.

"What do you think this is about, Ben?" Lori said, if only to avoid talking about Jennifer.

"Frankenstein," Ben said simply. "The Guardian Star. Whether we'll need to worry about end-of-year exams."

Deveraux's face appeared on the Briefing Room's imposing screen. "Thank you for assembling so promptly," he said. "We have little time to spare. I have to tell you that our sources in the military report that communications with the Guardian Star have been disrupted by unknown powers. Whatever is currently occurring aboard the space station is also unknown. Needless to say, none of this information has been or will be released to the general public, but we have to assume the worst."

"Really?" Eddie grunted. "A mind-controlled president and the deadliest array of weaponry ever in the history of the world at the mercy of a clone of Dr. Averill 'Don't Call Me Mad' Frankenstein. What's so bad about that?"

"Therefore," Deveraux was continuing, "we must take immediate action. A Deveraux shuttle is already being prepared for launch. Our remaining graduate teams are presently deployed across the globe and cannot be guaranteed to reach the launch site within the necessary time frame. Therefore, because of their prior knowledge of Dr. Frankenstein —"

Say it, urged Ben silently, the adrenaline already pumping. *Say it so everyone can hear.*

"— Bond Team will lead our assault on the Guardian Star, if such an assault becomes imperative."

Ben felt Lori squeezing his hand, but he derived greater pleasure at that moment from the jealous glance cast his way by Simon Macey.

"They will be accompanied by Corporal Keene and myself."

"What?" Had Ben heard right?

As if to ensure that he had: "I will be going with them," said Jonathan Deveraux.

"They're all against you, all of them."

President Graveney Westwood knew it. As he sat in the control center of the Guardian Star, surrounded by monitors, computers, and Frankenstein's men, his brow creased and his lip trembled with the knowledge.

"Even up here, even in space, they have been plotting against you, tempting you into a trap. You realize that, don't you?"

The president bowed his head. The eyes of the most powerful

man in the world had tears in them, and there was a sob in his throat.

"As for the others, the earth is teeming with your enemies. Now that you're gone, they're free to make their move against you. You can trust none of them. Nobody is your friend but me. Everyone is your enemy but me."

The president held his head in his hands and rocked like a baby. "Help me," he bleated. "Help me."

"Of course I'll help you. Look."

The president did. Twin cylindrical metal tubes rose from the floor, one slightly to the right of him, the other slightly to the left. Their rounded tops retracted automatically. The impression of a hand was revealed on each, the imprints glowing a peaceful green.

"You can save yourself, Mr. President. You can crush your enemies and save the world. You need only to activate the Guardian Star's weapons systems. You can see where your hands must go. And quickly, before your time runs out."

Obediently, the president pressed his hands into the green grooves. Immediately, the green became red. Red like blood, red like flame, red like destruction.

"Excellent," said Dr. Averill Frankenstein.

Of course, they'd flown missions in outer space before. *Virtual* outer space, Eddie had to admit, but the real thing couldn't be a great deal different. And they'd been subjected to G-forces, to the effects of sudden decompression, to survival techniques in a vacuum (and their special-issue shock suits came with quickly fitted oxygen-recycling masks and magnetic boots, anyway). So why was he finding strapping himself in and awaiting the shuttle's launch this nerve-wracking? He'd always said he'd go far one day. You couldn't get much farther than space. What was it called on that old, twentieth-century sci-fi series they still showed from time to time? The final frontier? Well, 'frontier' was fine. It was the use of the word 'final' that Eddie took issue with.

"These straps," he complained to Bex alongside him. "Any tighter and they'd cut off the flow of blood to the head."

"Only a problem if you've got a brain to keep oxygenated," Bex responded tartly.

"Oxygen what?"

"Precisely. Can you maybe just keep quiet for a bit, Eddie?"

"Sure, but it's just as well we didn't book the economy tour, I bet."

So Bex wasn't having a good time, either. Maybe she still didn't feel like part of the team. Maybe her parentage was going to be a problem, after all. Eddie knew she'd had a special audience with her father before they'd left for the launch site, and she'd not mentioned anything about it. It had probably been to prepare her for the strange luggage that Cally was carrying — Bex's dad was now a laptop. This whole affair was getting weirder by the minute.

Cally supposed she should be honored, her techno-skills qualifying her as first choice nursemaid for a fraction of the mind of Jonathan Deveraux, downloaded on to the computer she now stashed (carefully) beneath her seat. But it was a weighty responsibility. If events still unfolding meant that they had to board the Guardian Star, Cally's mission was to upload Deveraux on to the space station's own computer system so that he could override any instructions that Frankenstein might have programmed in. Specifically, anything involving weapons of mass destruction and their firing. If she failed in her task, for the people of Earth it'd be more than raindrops falling on their heads. Cally glanced toward Ben. He seemed so cool, so confident, so sure of himself. *But whoa, hold on a tad there, Cal,* she told herself. Surely she wasn't really wishing she was more like Benjamin T. Stanton Jr.?

Lori, on the other side of Ben, could imagine what was in his thoughts. Honor. Triumph. Glory. And not necessarily in that order. She wondered if there was any room in there for her. They were about to face a twisted maniac who'd almost killed them more than once already. The fate of the world itself might rest in their hands. And her hands would feel better if Ben was holding one of them — that little bit of reassurance. But his attention was fixed on the future, elsewhere. He wasn't aware of her or her needs. She could tell him, of course, but she shouldn't have to, should she?

Lori sighed slightly, turned away. She could see that Jake and Jennifer were not suffering from the same communication problem. At least, not the same kind.

"There's still time, Jen," Jake was urging. "This just isn't a good idea. I'm worried about you. We all are."

"No need, Jake." Jennifer refused to listen. "The medics couldn't find anything wrong with me. Mr. Deveraux himself gave permission for me to come with the rest of you, in case I remember something about Frankenstein that might be useful."

"He said it was a risk," Jake qualified. "He said if the situation wasn't so desperate . . . He left it up to you, Jen." His expression suggested her presence on the mission was hurting him somehow.

"But I feel good, Jake, I feel fine." For a dead secret agent somehow restored to life. "Unless you know something I don't." The best form of defense was attack.

"No, no," Jake denied, too quickly for truth. Guiltily. He knew, all right, they all did. Were they all sneaking glances at her now, waiting for her to puddle into protoplasm like Grant's clone? *No,* she commanded herself, squeezing her eyes shut to hide in the dark. *Paranoia wasn't allowed. Get a grip. Focus.*

"Jen? You're not . . . This is not good —"

"I'll be all right, Jake. Trust me." She appealed to him with remorseless green eyes. Jake could not stand against them. "Besides," — as the final countdown began to reverberate through the cabin and the shuttle stirred — "I think you could say we're committed."

"And so," Dr. Averill Frankenstein preened, fluttering his fingers like albino caterpillars, "I thought it would be generous of me to restore communications, update you on what has been happening so high above your heads."

Grant and a pair of Deveraux faces watched the screen grimly as Frankenstein gloated. In the background, they could see President Graveney Westwood, cringing and cowering in the commander's chair.

"I'm afraid your President Westwood has now lost what little mind he had. Effectively, I am now in total control of the Guardian Star and, indeed, the Guardian Star's weaponry, which I understand has never been used in anger." Frankenstein giggled.

"Laugh while you can, you madman," glowered Grant. "Our turn'll come."

"And if you people in authority would like that to remain

the case," the doctor pursued, "then I advise you to keep me happy. To repeat once again how that can be achieved: Money, lots of it. Twenty percent of the gross domestic product of the United States of America, I think. That should keep up my laboratories for a while. Oh, and I'd like a little island all to myself where I can pursue my work without interruption. Shall we say Hawaii? You don't need to say yes immediately. Think about it for a while. I've got to retrain the Guardian Star's missiles on your major cities, in any case. I'll be in touch again soon."

"Never's too soon," grumbled Grant.

"Oh, but in case you're considering something anti-social like an armed assault, I wouldn't want to be responsible for any *unnecessary* deaths." Frankenstein drummed his fingers against his lips. "Now let me see. Washington, I think, and Paris — I never did like the French — and perhaps London, not that Britain matters much any more . . ."

The broadcast flickered into blankness and silence. "Thank the Lord for that," sighed Grant, running his hands through his hair. "Sir?" He gazed up at Deveraux.

"The military will attack. With missiles. With men. They will certainly fail. We have no choice, Grant," said Deveraux. "Deploy Bond Team."

"I don't want to come on like Mr. Depresso," Eddie had said, "but exactly what's to stop Frankenstein from seeing us coming and simply blasting us into space dust?"

It has seemed like an important issue as the Earth spun away from them on its axis and blue views plunged into black, the G-forces abating as the Deveraux shuttle left the atmosphere and speared toward the Guardian Star. Not that survival had ever been anything less than a number-one priority for Eddie Nelligan.

"What's the matter, Nelligan?" Corporal Keene had grunted. "Do you want to live forever?"

"Maybe not forever, Corporal, sir," Eddie had lamented, "but I kind of hoped I'd make it to next week."

"The shuttle has SPIE technology," Keene had finally revealed. "Provided we don't get close enough for heat sensors to detect us, we'll be masked. Frankenstein won't even know we're there. Make you feel any better?"

It had done. Eddie had even begun to wish he'd brought a camera with him to take some shots of the distant Earth. The trouble was, like all good moods when you were a student at Spy High, it didn't last. The order to deploy had seen to that. Crunch time was coming.

They made their way smartly to the hangar deck where the Space-Spheres were stored. A number of techs were busy carrying out final systems checks. Eddie was dismayed at how fragile the transparent bubbles appeared, how worryingly thin the outer skin. "You don't have, like, any specially reinforced spheres by any chance, do you?" he asked one of the techs. From the bemused expression on the man's face, Eddie guessed not.

"Very well," Keene barked. "We have a job to do. You know what it is. You know how crucial it is. We board the Guardian Star, upload Mr. Deveraux on to its computer systems —" Cally had Mr. Deveraux strapped to her back — "and regain control. We put an end to this crisis. And if we happen to put an end to Dr. Frankenstein at the same time, well —" Keene smiled grimly — "sometimes espionage can be a wonderful thing. Into your spheres, people. We reach the drop zone in five minutes."

Now Ben did come to Lori, squeezed her hand. "You ready for this, Lo?" She could tell that he was. He almost seemed taller somehow, and his blue eyes sparkled with energy.

"Ready as I'll ever be," she said. "Kiss for luck?"

"Kiss, sure," Ben obliged. His lips were cold. "But you won't need luck. See you on the star, Lo."

"God, it's chilly enough already," Eddie moaned. "I hope these things are insulated."

"What's the problem, Ed?" Cally quipped, parting the skin of her Space-Sphere. "You generate plenty of hot air yourself."

"Oh, very funny, Cal, very amusing. Hey, Bex," Eddie pointed, "maybe we should have done a deal like Jake and Jen. What do you think?"

Jennifer's unexpected return to the team and her unfamiliarity with the Space-Spheres had forced the techs to customize one of them so that it could carry two people. If Jennifer and Jake weren't already close, they soon would be.

Bex watched Jake helping his partner into her harness and then attach his own. "What I think," she said, and not with enthusiasm, "is four minutes to the drop zone."

There was silence then, tense, expectant, as Bond Team and Corporal Keene secured themselves inside their spheres. Four minutes to the drop zone. And how long could they expect to last after that?

Three. As they telepathically activated the spheres, the psi-wires affixed to their foreheads, their self-contained environments bathed in yellow.

Two. As Jennifer pressed against Jake and he was glad because he could feel her living warmth and nothing would part them again. As Ben looked across to Bex and remembered her earlier failure in the spheres and knew that errors now would be fatal.

One. As the lights of the hangar deck dimmed and died. As the floor flashed red beneath them. As the jangle of the space lock announced its imminent opening.

"Deploy! Deploy!" A grating voice, a mechanized voice.

And the spacelock parting like lips. A gulf below the sphere, a chasm, a yawning void, the emptiness of illimitable space. Someone screamed.

The Space-Spheres spilled into impossible blackness.

"Oh, my God! Oh, my God!" This wasn't Training Chamber Four. This was a chamber without walls. Eddie felt himself falling, head over heels, no way of telling which way was up or down, no way *was* up or down. He couldn't find direction, couldn't find control. He was plummeting, plunging. The yellow glow of his sphere flickered like a faulty lightbulb as his concentration crumbled. If it wasn't for his harness, he'd have been helplessly dashed against the skin of the sphere. Eddie was on the brink of panic.

"Stabilize your spheres!" Keene's voice in his ear, defying anyone to disobey him. "That means now! All of you!"

Eddie had needed to hear the corporal's uncompromising tones. They came like a slap to a hysteric. *Stabilize. Concentrate. Assert yourself.* It wasn't his fate to fall to Earth, to flare briefly in the atmosphere like a struck match. He'd never get off with Bex if that happened.

Eddie slowed the sphere's descent, braked its tumble, smoothed the movement into a swoop and a climb, found himself upright again and able to remain that way. The power of his mind had mastered the sphere. And his teachers back in kindergarten had called him brainless!

"Nelligan, are you thinking of joining us any time soon?" Keene summoned.

"Be right with you, Corporal, sir," Eddie said. A distance away, he detected the glimmer of the others' spheres like trainee meteors. His own sphere's guidance systems would take him directly to them. "It's just like Disneyland, isn't it?"

Hardly, thought Lori, hearing her teammate. Nothing manufactured, nothing artificial, could possibly match the beauty of her surroundings now. The tranquility of the boundless cosmos, the blackness that was as perfect as polished ebony, the rivers of stars rippling across the dark, the breathtaking Earth, an exotic bead of glass, and the shuttle, poised in the currents of space like a shark. "It's magnificent," she murmured.

"We're not here to admire the view, Angel." Keene again, living up to his name. "All we need to see is the Guardian Star. Picture it in your minds, and let the guidance systems do the rest."

Seven circles of light in search of a space station.

It was Jake who saw them first. "Heads up! Incoming!"

Eddie groaned for them all. "Ah, Corporal Keene, sir? Those long white things heading our way, they're not missiles by any chance, are they?"

"Interceptors," Keene identified. "But hold your course. We're too small a target for them to have picked up."

In the silent vacuum of space, the arrow-shaped missiles passed Bond Team serenely by, like smears of chalk on an endless blackboard. The spheres trembled as if in fear of their proximity.

"So assuming they're not just out for some exercise," Cally said, "what are they intercepting?"

"We're not the only ones making an assault on the Guardian Star," Keene noted grimly.

"Behind us. Look!" Lori had gazed ahead of the missiles' apparent trajectory. She'd seen them, glittering gray ghosts in the distance. More missiles, though these she knew would be carrying government markings and were heading toward them. She also knew they'd never arrive.

When the collision came, Lori expected noise. She expected an explosion that would deafen and pulverize her ears, a cataclysm of sound like the end of the world. But there was nothing, of course. All snuffed out by the airless void, extinguished like it didn't matter, as if nothing could matter out here in infinity. Just brief flares of light, mute fireworks flashing yellow and red.

"Is that it? Is that the best they can manage?" Ben gaped in disbelief. "Earth's best defense? Picked off without Frankenstein even having to try?"

"Desperation," Keene observed. "It's still down to us, people. And hold on. We could be in for a bumpy ride."

A shock wave. It smashed into the Space-Spheres with sweeping and unstoppable strength, the aftermath of the explosions, sending the fragile bubbles careering hectically along with it. Lori fought to retain even a semblance of psi-control of her sphere, ramming her eyes shut, and praying that when she opened them again she wouldn't see a tear in the fabric of the skin, black space reaching in with icy fingers to pluck her out. Her gauntlets and stirrups strained; even in her harness, she felt battered and bruised, dazed and disoriented. But she had to keep her focus, keep the sphere's life-support systems functioning. Ignore the pain. Reject the fear. The granite force of the shock wave could not last much longer.

"Is everybody okay?" Keene's voice, as equilibrium was gradually restored.

Everybody was okay. Lori spoke her name in turn, opened her eyes. The other way around and she'd probably not have been able to say anything. Perversely, the shock wave had done them a favor. The Guardian Star circled before them. Up close now, it was huge, imposing, powerful. *Deadly,* Lori thought. And at its heart, somewhere in the control center, a final reckoning with Averill Frankenstein awaited.

"Now we've just got to find our way in," observed Ben.

"Or not," said Eddie hopefully. "Look at that." Apertures in the circumference of the space station's wheel opened. "How helpful is that? I take back everything I said about Dr. Frankenstein."

Then, from within the dark interior, satellites swarmed like metallic wasps, scarcely bigger than the Space-Spheres themselves but wickedly spiked, the tips of their steel antennae flashing angry red as targets were detected. Seven of them. The satellites swooped to attack, and now the antennae blazed bolts of laser fire.

"Drones!" Keene had obviously been doing his homework. "The last line of defense. Designed to pick off any survivors of a failed assault."

"I guess we qualify," gulped Cally.

"I take back what I said about taking back what I said about . . ." Eddie decided he'd be better off activating his sphere's own defense systems. "Oh, forget it. Watch out, guys!"

The drones' bolts stabbed close, their brightness intensified by the prevailing black. But here was the beauty of telepathic power, Ben considered. He only had to think of a maneuver and his Space-Sphere could accomplish it. The drones were fast but no machine could match the speed of a human brain, particularly one as finely trained as his own. As long as his instincts and his wits remained sure, he could more than take the fight to his attackers.

A psi-bolt coalesced at the front of his sphere, sparkled, struck. The nearest drone disintegrated. Another took its place. Ben evaded its lasers, rose above it, fired another psi-bolt. Score two for Space Ace Stanton.

But the Guardian Star was disgorging drones in such numbers that they would soon be surrounded. Not even Ben had eyes in the back of his head.

"Come together!" Keene barked. (Ben had just been going to suggest that.) "Watch each other's backs!" (That, too.)

Seven became one. The Space-Spheres formed a single shape, a larger globe to fend off the drones' assault. A barrage of psi-bolts tore into the satellites' less organized ranks, making teamwork count. And all the while, the Guardian Star loomed nearer.

"If we make it inside the wheel, we're safe," Keene encouraged. "The drones are programmed not to fire when doing so might damage their base."

The space station's outer rim arced above them like a ring of Saturn. Eddie, closest to it, saw the corridor spokes linking the wheel to the hub, saw the docking bays and the presidential shuttle already in. "We're gonna make it." With a euphoria born of disbelief. "This is gonna work. Bex . . ." He wanted to tell her the good news, but he never did.

Bex's sphere was still within the drones' range. And as she approached the rotating wheel, a stray laser bolt somehow got through her psi-defenses. Somehow, it struck her sphere head-on.

"Bex!" Horror among her teammates.

Nobody saw the Space-Sphere burst, that was something. Nobody saw Bex's body. But they heard her scream and then the light of her sphere went out and in their communicators, they could hear nothing. The silence was worse than the scream.

Eddie thought he saw her sphere, but it was difficult to be sure in the darkness of space. It seemed to be dropping away from the others, falling into nowhere, into nothingness, a stone sinking into the depths of an uncharted sea. Going and gone.

"We've got to get after her!" he urged. "She could still be alive, just unconscious or . . . Come on, what are we waiting for?" His Space-Sphere quivered for pursuit.

"As you were, Nelligan." If Keene felt any emotion concerning the sudden loss of one of his students, his tone did not betray it. "If Deveraux's alive, she'll have to help herself. If she's not, we can't help her anyway. You're on a mission, Bond Team. Listen to your training. Only the mission matters."

"Yeah? Well, sometimes our training stinks." But Eddie held his position after all.

Jennifer was as stunned as her teammates, but in her mind, it wasn't Bex falling through space but herself, and above her not the Guardian Star but a man in a scaled skin. And she knew his name now. And that he'd killed her. She knew it, but she didn't quite remember it all. Not yet. A bead of thick, milky sweat trickled into her eye.

"We're there, Jen," Jake was saying. "Any minute and we're out of this thing."

Jennifer felt that she wanted that. She wanted it very much.

Keene directed them toward one of the docking bays. With so many spheres requiring access to the Guardian Star at once, a single airlock wouldn't do. Ben could see that, didn't disagree, but it did occur to him that Corporal Keene was taking rather a lot of charge of the operation, when Ben Stanton had actually been duly elected the leader of Bond Team. All right, so Keene outranked him, was older (a lot), and more experienced, but even so. Ben didn't like to feel that someone else was taking over.

So he watched sullenly as the corporal's sphere clung to the side of the docking bay like a limpet, accessing and activating the entry mechanisms. He looked on as the bay dutifully opened, offering a glimpse of the dock within: steel gantries, red lights, and the promise of an atmosphere. He floated in with the others but half-hoped that Keene would not be following. No such luck.

The docking bay resealed itself, and oxygen pumped in to fill the temporary vacuum. Green lights flashed to signal safety. The intruders stripped off their Space-Spheres like winter clothes on the first warm day of spring.

"Am I glad to get out of that," Lori spoke for them all.

"This is no time to relax, people," Keene reminded them — unnecessarily, Ben thought. "Check your sleepshot. We've got to keep moving before Frankenstein's men can locate us."

"Ah, Corporal Keene, sir?" Eddie raised his hand nervously, like a small child in class needing to use the bathroom. "I think they already have."

On the gantries above them, ringing and encircling them, gray-uniformed, grim-faced men with laser rifles.

"Don't do anything stupid!" warned one of them coldly. "You're coming with us."

CHAPTER FOURTEEN

"Okay," said Eddie, "so what qualifies as anything stupid?"

"If we surrender now, we've had it," Ben gloomed.

"Lie down on the floor!" Instructions from above. "Spread your arms and legs!"

"I'm not sure this is the time for that," muttered Cally.

"Don't worry," growled Jake. "I'm not lying down for these guys. Sir?" To Keene.

"Open fire!" The corporal showed he meant it, drawing and blazing away with his shock blaster in one lightning move. The gantry crackled with sparks, startling Frankenstein's men with the suddenness of the attack. "Choose your marks. Scatter!"

Keene was right (again). Use the enemy's numbers against them. Ben was on one knee immediately, arm extended, sleepshot pumping from his wristband. So there were more bad guys than there were Bond Teamers. That meant there were more of them to hit, particularly as they were bunched together so closely up there on the gantry, lined up like targets at a shooting gallery. Ben wondered what the prize was for the highest score. As his first victim was knocked backward against the wall and his second clattered to the floor, he thought he might be in with a chance.

The good thing about sleepshot was that even a nick from one of the shells would be enough to induce oblivion for hours. Anybody struck by sleepshot was no longer any kind of threat. A wound from a laser rifle, on the other hand, and you could still keep fighting. Theoretically. Not that Ben felt like testing the idea out for real, though it dawned on him that he might have to. Frankenstein's men were beginning to find their range.

And here was the problem. As they reduced the ranks of their attackers, the remainder became harder to hit, and the quality of their marksmanship was improving accordingly. Bond Team was firing up, at a foe partially protected by the steel of the gantry. While the enemy was firing down — which was easier — at targets protected only by half a dozen transparent bubbles. Ben sensed the odds were shifting, and not in their favor.

Jake and Jennifer were pinned down behind a Space-Sphere. Laser bolts sizzled at the metal floor around them. They stabbed through the sphere's skin, deflating it like an old balloon. Soon, there would be no shelter at all.

"Jen, help me!" Jake was firing with both wristbands, his fists punching the air as if in victory. "Use your sleepshot. We've got to fight!"

Fight? But the chaos, the clamor, the confusion, it was all too much for her. Jennifer huddled up by the sphere, felt a need to curl herself up into the security of a ball. It was too bright, too loud — overwhelming. She couldn't fight. She'd fought once before, and where had that gotten her? She could almost see Talon again. He was coming for her once more, and this time there'd be no escape.

A last thought that was in Lori's mind, too — escape and its likelihood. Not much of one. A laser bolt seared her eyeballs and instinctively she threw herself to one side. Her shock suit hung raggedly at her knee, the fabric torn but her flesh unblemished. But if her reflexes had been just a fraction slower. . . . *Don't let difficulties distract you,* Lori reminded herself. *Focus on solutions.* And she might just have one.

From this angle, Lori could see the bad guys' boots. They were not magnetic. Bond Team's and Corporal Keene's were. Going out into space without magnetic boots was like venturing into a storm without an umbrella.

Lori thought she might make it rain.

"Ben!" she called. "Cover me!"

Her tone of voice meant he didn't need to ask why. He simply did so, raking the gantry with sleepshot as Lori hurtled toward . . . where? With white bolts blasting in her path and the steel floor erupting around her. Where did she think she was going? And then Ben realized where. And why.

The docking bay's controls. Perhaps it *was* getting a little stuffy in here.

"Masks and boots!" Ben yelled. "Now!"

As Lori activated the docking bay's opening mechanism and a sliver of space appeared like a black grin. As the helpless air was sucked out with an almost visible rush.

Frankenstein's goons panicked, not unreasonably. They didn't have magnetic boots to anchor them to the metal floor. They didn't have oxygen-recycling masks to help them cope in a vacuum. And it was unlikely that any of their future travel ambitions included drifting forever into outer space. They tried to make it to the secondary airlock while they could, to seek refuge in the main body of the Guardian Star. The docking bay didn't seem to want them to go. It yanked them back like they were on ropes, tugged them off balance, bumped them along the gantry, down the metal stairways. They were morsels about to be munched by the mouth of the void. Bond Team watched as Frankenstein's lackeys, gasping and grabbing at their throats, bounced past them, dragged by invisible forces to the brink of space. Their eyes and veins were bulging. The vacuum would turn them inside out.

But not even they deserved a fate as grisly as that. They were only hired help, after all. Lori worked at the controls again. The docking bay pressed its lips together once more, perhaps a little ruefully. Oxygen returned.

The handful of Frankenstein's men who still retained their consciousness were relieved of that burden by sleepshot. "It'll save them worrying about what might have just happened to them," Cally said considerately, following the others' example and removing her no longer necessary air-recycling mask.

"You're all heart, Cal," noted Eddie.

"Heart has no place in the field," Keene observed, though not harshly, "and neither does delay. Let's go."

They passed through the secondary airlock watchfully, but nobody was waiting in the corridor they entered. It stretched out to the left and right of them, slightly curved in keeping with the circularity of the Guardian Star's hub. "This place is sending me around the bend already," said Eddie, sleepshot poised just in case.

Corporal Keene pressed a stud in his belt buckle and the microchip inside produce a three-dimensional hologram of the space station, their present location identified by a cluster of red dots. *Now he's going to give us our orders,* Ben brooded, *when we already know exactly what we've got to do.* The presence of Keene on the mission was like a parent accompanying him on a date, an unnecessary encumbrance.

The control center was several levels above them. "Frankenstein will be expecting us to make for that," Keene reasoned, "and we wouldn't want to disappoint him, would we?" Almost a chuckle there. "So. Stanton, Angel, Daly, Chen, you're one team. Head for the control center. Make a lot of noise while you're doing it. Keep Frankenstein's forces occupied."

"Why?" Ben sounded more confrontational than he'd intended. "What are you going to be doing, sir?"

"Myself, Cross, and Nelligan will be another team. And we'll be doing what's *not* expected. Heading here." Keene dipped his finger into the hologram. "The computer network center." Only three levels below. "We have an extra program to add to their server, don't we, Cross?"

Cally felt the laptop still secured to her back. "Mr. D.'s ready and waiting, sir."

"So we're just the diversion?" Ben's resentment could be reached out and touched.

Lori wished he'd not said anything, not now.

"There's no such thing as *just* a diversion in the field, Stanton," Keene rebuked. "We're part of a team, and everyone has a job to do. Do yours. We'll reinforce you once Mr. Deveraux has neutralized Frankenstein's weapons capability." He pressed the belt stud a second time and the hologram dribbled away like a chalk drawing in the rain. "Good luck."

He headed left, Cally and Eddie close behind. "Good luck to you, too," Ben muttered. All part of a team. Right. So why did he feel like he'd just been relegated to the subs' bench? It didn't do his confidence much good when he glanced at Jake and Jennifer, either. Jen was looking weird, spaced out, a liability, and if Jake was paying too much attention to her, compromising his concentration, well, at least he could still rely on Lori.

Who was regarding him searchingly. "Are we waiting for Frankenstein's goons to come find us?"

"No. Guess not." Ben focused. "Okay, so what did Keene say? Let's make some noise."

"Remarkable. Astonishing." Frankenstein pressed his face against the screen to make doubly sure, but the grainy footage of the altercation in the docking bay did not lie. "It's really them. Again. And that charming clone, too. Gene chambers, death traps, treacherous tutors, whatever I do to dissuade them they *insist* on staying alive. And they insist on interfering with my plans. The impudence of youth, I suppose." He leaned back and curled his fingers together like knotting ropes. "What do you think I should do with them, Mr. President?"

President Graveney Westwood, from his quivering slump in the commander's chair, had only one response in what remained of his mind. "Enemies . . . kill the enemies . . . they're all around us . . . kill them . . ."

"Yes, thank you, Mr. President, for that erudite analysis." But of course, Westwood did have a point. Frankenstein reviewed his position. He was well defended here in the control center. The Guardian Star's missiles were locked on to their target cities earthside. And he had plenty of expendable lackeys still at his disposal. Perhaps he'd better make them earn their wages. "Captain," he beckoned.

"Yes, sir?"

"Those young people — I don't want them to get much older . . ."

"Did I tell you the one about this place sending me around the bend?" Eddie asked as he struggled to keep up with Cally ar Corporal Keene.

"Yes," Cally returned, "and it wasn't funny the first time."

"Statement of fact," Eddie grumbled. They'd been following the curve of the corridor for longer than he'd thought possible. "We go much farther, we'll be back where we started. Did I tell you the one about how this place has got me running around in circles?"

"Did I tell you the one about 'Shut up, Nelligan, before you get us all killed'?" Keene paused, raised his hand for the students to follow suit.

"Now that you mention it, Corporal Keene, sir —"

"Shut up, Nelligan, before you get us all killed."

Eddie saw what Keene had seen, or rather *who*. A quartet of candidates for the getting-us-all-killed role. The sighting was mutual. Frankenstein's men were slow. Cally and Eddie were firing sleepshot before they could even bring their laser rifles to bear. Four groans and four thuds. Corporal Keene's shock blaster not required.

"Good shooting, huh, Corporal?" Eddie fished for praise.

"Competent, Nelligan. I'd expect no less from a Deveraux trainee."

Deveraux. Bex. For a second, her absence had slipped Eddie's mind. He shut up guiltily.

"All right." Keene stepped over the fallen goons' bodies unceremoniously. "We've reached the elevator that should take us ectly into the computer center. Straight down. For Nelligan's t, no more running around in circles."

e they should have been more alert then. Corporal t making a witty comment, that should have re- expect the unexpected. Keene operated the el- open.

Three more of Frankenstein's men were inside. Their laser rifles poked at the intruders' chests, like fingers saying, "I told you so."

"No sudden moves, please," instructed the goon in the middle, "or we'll cut you in two. And back against the wall."

"We've always got our backs against the wall," bemoaned Eddie, obeying anyway.

The three men emerged into the corridor. "Dr. Frankenstein will be pleased." Their leader was smiling. And then he wasn't. He was collapsing in a heap on the floor.

"I wouldn't bet on it."

The second lackey dropped, and the third. Cally could see the sleepshot shells buried in their cheeks. She looked to the sound of the newcomer's voice.

"Bex!" Eddie couldn't restrain himself. It was Bex. She was all right. Better yet, she was *there.* Surely no one could begrudge him a hug under those circumstances. "You're alive!" He seized her, swung her around.

"Yeah, for now, Eddie," Bex laughed, "but if you squeeze any harder, I might need medical attention."

"Just call me *Dr.* Nelligan."

"Bex." Cally was smiling, too. "Eddie, do you mind?" Virtually pulling him off so that she could hug her teammate in her turn. "I knew you'd make it, Bex. It's so good to see you."

"Corporal Keene?" Bex grinned, opening her arms. "Wanna make it a full house?"

"A timely intervention, Deveraux," gruffed Keene, which probably meant no. "Obviously, you managed to regain contro[l] of your Space-Sphere."

"With a little help," Bex said. "I'll tell you later." As b

Cally and Eddie looked quizzical. "Yeah, so I found myself a nice, out-of-the-way airlock, snuck inside, and thought I'd better rejoin the mission."

"In that case," Keene said, indicating the open elevator, "shall we?"

Ben's team hadn't taken the elevators. They'd climbed several levels via the steep spiral stairway that wrapped around the inner hub of the Guardian Star, and they'd climbed quickly, eager to put space between them and their teammates. "Draw Frankenstein's goons away," Ben said grudgingly.

"Nice idea, but I don't see anyone following us, goon or otherwise." Lori was looking at empty corridors in both directions. "I suppose that's a first, secret agents *wanting* to make contact with the enemy."

"Guess here's your chance, Lo." Jake indicated a spy camera set high up on the wall and focused on the door to the stairwell. He waved provocatively. "Hey, Frankenstein, you watching? It's us. We're coming to get you, you hear? And hey, Jennifer's with us, too. She's back on our side where she belongs. What do you think of that?"

There was no way of telling, of course, though if Jake had been less occupied with the camera, he might have noticed that nnifer herself seemed less than happy. Lori saw it. She saw fer wincing, touching her brow with trembling fingers as if a sudden migraine. Her skin color seemed unhealthy ed. The green of her eyes was fading.

u okay?"

th hands now, rubbing at her temples. "I can't y head, I can't stand it. Jake . . ."

"It's all right, Jen. I'm here." Frankenstein forgotten. For a second.

"You're not the only one." The warning in Ben's tone told them everything. They'd finally been found. Uniformed hirelings stampeded toward them, laser rifles blasting. "If Frankenstein ever engaged guys who could shoot straight, we'd be in real trouble." Ben crouched down. Sleepshot sent the lead goon tumbling.

Lori dropped to one knee beside Ben, fired her own sleepshot. The bodies were piling up. "I can do this all day," she observed.

"Hopefully you won't need to." Ben called to Jake and Jennifer. "You two feel like joining the party any time soon?"

Unlikely. Jennifer was shuddering now like she'd been plunged into deep cold water, and a lost, desolate wail rose from her throat. Talon, the scaled man was inside her head. He'd forced his way back, he'd *clawed* his way back into her brain, and she could see him, and she knew him, and she *remembered* what he'd done. Jake was trying to hold her, calm her, futile in the crackle of lasers and the shouts of combat. She was struggling in his arms because she was sure it wasn't Jake but Talon. She *remembered* him killing her. She *remembered* her final breath and the darkness flooding over her. And she *remembered* dying. And now she could feel herself dying again.

Ben: "What's going on?"

Lori: "Ben, we've got to help her!"

Frankenstein's men advancing in spite of their losses.

Jennifer in desperate strength pushing Jake away, crying ou in despair, turning and running, fleeing, from Jake, from the b tle, from everything.

"Jen!" Jake made to pursue her, and a ricocheting laser slashed at his thigh. He fell against the corridor wall in a

"Jake, no!" Lori turned, too, snatched from the fighting by her concern for Jake. Not for long. Moments only. But moments were enough.

Her concentration was broken. The line of defense was broken. All of a sudden, Frankenstein's men were crowding in and sleepshot was no longer an answer. The three members of Bond Team were surrounded.

With a resentful glance at Lori and the wounded Jake, Ben did the thing he hated most in all the world. He surrendered.

"Sorry, Mr. Computer Operator Person," said Cally politely, "but I need access to the server a tad more than you do." She heaved the man's white-coated body out of her way and settled herself into what had evidently been his chair. The operator didn't object. But then, people with sleepshot shells studding the back of their neck rarely did. He looked nice and peaceful lying there on the floor.

His equally comatose colleagues sprawled around the computer network center in a variety of postures. "It's kind of like musical chairs, isn't it?" Eddie remarked. "If I start humming, you think they'll make a move again?"

"Nelligan," growled Corporal Keene, "can you repress your inct for idiocy at least until Cross has done her job? We may ot in here easily enough —" as the unconscious forms of icians and a handful of guards testified — "but as soon ein realizes where we are, he's likely to send men. raux cover the elevator doors. If they open, 's inside."

al Keene, sir." Eddie did his best to look

vigilant. "Back as a team, Bex," he grinned. "Makes you feel good, doesn't it?"

"Oh yeah, Eddie. Ecstatic." Bex sighed. "How are we doing there, Cal? Is my dad okay?"

"I hope so." Cally already had the laptop open and was connecting it to the server. A few seconds to boot up and she'd be in a position to add Mr. Jonathan Deveraux to the Guardian Star's software.

"Time frame," demanded Keene.

"Very, very soon," supplied Cally, a little resentfully. If the corporal thought he could upload Mr. Deveraux any faster . . .

"Can we maybe get an extra 'very' in there, Cal?" Eddie called from the elevator. "As in, like, immediately." He outstretched his arms in readiness.

"We've got company," Bex explained. The indicator flashed above the elevator door. "I doubt they're bearing gifts." Her own wristband gleamed as she, too, prepared to fire.

"You know what to do," snapped Keene. "Continue, Cross. I'll watch your back."

Sleepshot whoever's inside. Eddie didn't have a problem with that. Until the elevator doors slid open and he saw who *was* inside.

Some of Frankenstein's goons, yes, but they weren't alone. They had the remainder of Bond Team with them, laser rifles nuzzling under their chins like contented cats. Eddie and Bex stared helplessly. Outmaneuvered.

Corporal Keene half thought about making a stand. The other half thought prevailed. Only the mission mattered, true, but not even he could willfully sacrifice the lives of so many of his students.

And Cally, who was only seconds away from rousing Jonathan Deveraux to his work had no choice but to stop, too.

"Wristbands on the floor and hands on your heads. It's all over."

Cally leaned back in her seat despairingly. A guard tore the laptop's connecting wire from the server, took possession of the computer itself. "I suppose it's no good asking if I can hold it?" she said forlornly.

All over. And maybe it was.

At least Frankenstein seemed pleased to see them. "Come along in, my fine young friends," he beckoned as they were marched into the control center. "And Corporal Keene, too, is it? A pleasure to make your acquaintance, sir, even though that pleasure will, I fear, be brief. Bring them down here, men."

Frankenstein indicated an open area close to the room's rank of viewing screens, which at present transmitted images of the Guardian Star's missiles, jabbing into space like fingers pointing the way to Earth. "And that's right. Keep them covered and keep your distance. Their suits could give you a nasty shock otherwise."

"You'd better believe it," said Ben defiantly.

"Who are they? Dr. Averill, who are these people?" The whimpering tones of the most powerful man in the world, politically speaking, drew Bond Team's attention. President Graveney Westwood cowered behind the commander's chair, peeping above it like a World War I soldier in the trenches. "Don't let them near me. They want to hurt me. Kill them, Dr. Averill, kill them at once."

Frankenstein considered. "At once? Perhaps not. Perhaps their valiant efforts at survival merit the reward of witnessing my final triumph, after all."

"You're too kind," muttered Lori.

"Besides," Frankenstein addressed the Bond Teamers, "with all of you my helpless prisoners, I . . ." Something registered. "Captain, the Chinese girl, Jennifer Chen, why is she not with her teammates?"

The captain had to admit that the Chinese girl, Jennifer Chen, remained at liberty.

"Don't tell us," said Eddie, "but we've got men still searching for her, and she won't get far, etc."

"You see, Frankenstein?" Jake jibed. "Shocks come in all kinds of ways."

The doctor steepled his fingers and spoke calmly. "Well, let dear Jennifer run around a bit. She probably needs the exercise after all that time in a grave. And what can she do on her own when the seven of you failed to disrupt my schedule together? But keep looking for her, Captain. Loose ends are like untied shoelaces. They can trip you up."

"We found this, sir." The captain passed Frankenstein the laptop. "They were trying to upload something from it on to the computer system."

"Indeed?" Frankenstein held the object to his ear and shook it. "I wonder why."

"Get your goons to put their guns down, and we'll tell you," Ben offered.

"Oh, I don't think that'll be necessary, Benjamin. I think I can guess." The high-pitched giggle. "Are you in there, Mr. Deveraux? Keeping an eye on your students? Planning on stealing control of my lovely missiles from me, hmm? Well, we'll see about that." He placed the laptop on the floor. "Captain, your laser rifle, if you please." The captain obliged.

"No, don't kill me, Dr. Averill. Please! I beg you!" From behind the commander's chair.

"Shut up, Mr. President," said Frankenstein, "and good-bye, Mr. Deveraux. If you prefer to look away, my dear, I quite understand."

Bex didn't. She preferred to look straight ahead. No emotion registered on her face.

Frankenstein fired the laser rifle. The laptop fried.

"You can't stop me, Mr. Deveraux." Frankenstein's lips peeled back in a twisted parody of a smile. "Nobody can. Not you admirably persistent children up here. Not those staggeringly inept morons down on Earth. They attacked me, you know. They had the temerity to send missiles against Dr. Averill Frankenstein. Well, I have a surprise for them and a last little highlight for you, my young friends, before you reacquaint yourself with deep space, without life support this time, of course. The missiles you see on the screens, they are primed, and they are locked on to major targets across the globe. Time to blow away a few cobwebs, don't you think?"

Frankenstein pressed a button. Above the viewing screens, a number appeared. Sixty. Then it changed. Fifty-nine. Fifty-eight.

"A countdown," Frankenstein informed needlessly. "We've seen them before, haven't we? Only this time, this one," the giggle reached a new pitch of intensity, "nothing can stop it now!"

CHAPTER FIFTEEN

Anxious glances. No need for words. As the countdown continued on its blithe, untroubled way toward zero, Bond Team knew they had to do *something*. It was getting to the specifics that was a bit of a problem.

Fifty . . .

Ringed by rifles. They could attack, Ben gauged, throw themselves at their captors in a single, reckless charge. Some of them wouldn't get too far, that much would be certain, but one or two of his teammates (plus himself) might get through, might be able to overpower Frankenstein, arrest the countdown. Might.

Forty-five . . .

Might not. Jake was up for it, muscles so tensed and bunched they were almost straining at his shock suit. There was a dark fire in his eyes like he didn't care. But to surrender their own lives wouldn't help anybody. The spy who survived played the percentages. Heroic failure looked dramatic but didn't save the day.

Forty . . .

What was left of it.

Bex alone among the team seemed calm, almost tranquil. Almost like she was watching a movie and trusted the director against all the odds to deliver a happy ending.

Keene tried the you-don't-really-want-to-do-this tack, much loved by cops talking suicides off of rooftops. "Frankenstein, think of what you're doing, all the lives that'll be lost if you fire those missiles, innocent lives." Ben doubted it'd work.

"I am thinking of it," Frankenstein responded, momentarily grave. "It's making me feel all warm and cozy inside. It reminds me of a joke, too — a little bit of humor to release the tension. What do you call a million people atomized in one go?" The doctor giggled. "A good start." Bond Team were stone-faced. "No? Oh, well, suit yourselves."

Twenty . . .

It was too late, already too late. Panic snapped like a wild animal at Ben's brain. Surely not even Cally would be able to avert the computer-directed disaster now. All their training, all their trials, where had it all got them? To a grandstand view of the end of the world. Not quite what Ben had been hoping for.

Ten . . .

And Bex was kind of nodding now, like someone who knew what was going on. "Bex?" Ben frowned. "What's the matter with you?" She smiled serenely at him. She'd lost it, he realized with shock. Couldn't cope. Her mind had gone. So much for Deveraux's daughter. If it did come to a fight, they wouldn't be able to rely on Bex.

Five . . .

But the matter was irrelevant. It wouldn't come to a fight. Not now. In four seconds, Frankenstein — *three seconds* — would have won and it'd be good-bye Bond Team — *two* — and good-bye world.

One . . .

Ben held his breath for zero. He almost closed his eyes, too. But that would have been a sign of cowardice. Even at the end you had to . . .

One . . .

Not zero. One. Still one. Remaining one while the seconds in the real world raced by, intent to get on like the reader of a book eager for the final page.

One . . .

Frankenstein was not giggling now. His elongated fingers made question marks in the air. "What?" he blustered. "What?"

"What a pity for you, Frankenstein," came the voice of Jonathan Deveraux. "So near, yet so far." And it came from the mouth of Bex.

"You?" Frankenstein seemed to have been reduced to monosyllables, and baffled ones at that. He pointed to the still-smoking laptop. "But I killed you."

"It's not easy to kill a Deveraux," said the father, "but stopping a Frankenstein, on the other hand, is child's play. For example . . ."

The computers in the control center took their cue. They exploded, sparks and spouts of electricity stabbing outward and showering the room like shards of crackling glass. Bond Team took their cue, too. So they didn't have a clue what was going on. So what? Sudden diversions were a spycraft staple. If you wanted to stay alive, you used them.

Bond Team wanted to stay alive.

They were pouncing on their guards while the men were still shaken by the computers' apparent rebellion. Shock suits powered up, delivering electric, paralyzing blows. There was no defense. Bond Team channeled all their anger and rage and frustration into their fists, into their feet. They battled with chilling focus and bludgeoning intensity — a blur of precision training. The fight was over almost before it had begun.

Only Bex had stood aloof, smiling quietly to herself. Her

teammates quickly turned back to her, now both delighted and bemused. "Bex," thrilled Eddie, "was that major league ventriloquism or what?"

"Explanations later," came Jonathan Deveraux's voice. "Frankenstein first."

Of course. They wheeled. Ben cursed himself for his carelessness, doubly so when he surveyed the control center. A generous heap of insensate goons, Corporal Keene at the side of a blubbering President Westwood, but of Dr. Averill Frankenstein, no sign.

He had to have some work done on his internal organs. A stronger pair of lungs for a start. Then he might be able to run that little bit faster, reach the escape pod that little bit sooner. His lackeys might slow those wretched children down, but they wouldn't be able to stop them. They'd be pursuing him very shortly, he knew that. An athlete's lungs, that was what he wanted, and maybe an athlete's legs as well, in case such an undignified situation as this should arise again. Oh, well, recloning parts of his body, it'd give him something to do when he returned to his hidden labs earthside. Which, Frankenstein giggled, wouldn't be long now.

Fingers squirming in triumph, he accessed the escape pod.

It wasn't as plush as the presidential shuttle, true, but it was smaller, easier to pilot, and faster — designed for emergency evacuation purposes. The perfect way out. Frankenstein initiated the launch procedures and buckled himself in. Through the viewport he could see the spacelock open and the inviting freedom of infinite blackness beyond. He braced himself as the launch lights flashed.

The escape pod shot into the void like a bullet from a gun.

He'd done it. Evaded capture, avoided humiliation. So his plan hadn't worked out. There were other plans. He was a never-say-die sort of guy, quite literally. Frankenstein giggled and waved his candle fingers at the Guardian Star as it receded into the vast distance. Those annoying children would never catch him now.

Earth on the horizon, but it was probably better to take no chances while still in space. He ought to put a suit on. They were hanging at the back of the pod. Frankenstein unbuckled himself, sauntered across, chose a spacesuit like a customer at a gentleman's outfitters. Reached out for the suit.

The hand that reached out from behind it grabbed his bony wrist first.

"Hi," said Jennifer Chen, emerging from her hiding place. "I think we need to talk."

"Don't bother with the compliments," Cally grinned. "Just throw money." She was sitting at a console in the control center. She'd worked hard over the past few minutes, and the computer systems aboard the Guardian Star were now as docile as a pet animal. Maybe a cat. You could almost hear them purring. "Houston, we no longer have a problem."

"Weapons deactivated? Communications reestablished with earth?" Keene ticked them off from a mental list.

"You could even book tickets for the Super Bowl," Cally declared.

"Yeah? So what's that, Cal?" Ben directed her attention to the viewing screens. "The ball?" The escape pod. "And I don't think we need to be computer geniuses to guess who's aboard that and doing a runner. Too late for overrides now, I guess. Maybe we should just forget the throwing money bit, what do you think?"

Cally flushed slightly. "I can track him from here. Don't worry, Ben, we won't lose him."

Behind Cally and Ben, the other members of Bond Team were grouped around Bex. She'd suddenly seemed to be struck with dizziness, slight disorientation, and they'd helped her into the commander's chair. "I'm all right. I'm fine." Bex dismissed their concerns with a weary smile. "Honestly." She spoke once more in her own voice.

"You certainly sound more like yourself," approved Lori.

"Just as well," said Eddie, relievedly. "I don't think I could have appeared in public with a girl with a voice that low. People would talk."

"So what's the story, Bex?" Jake wanted to know. "How come your dad could intervene like that?"

"Plan B," said Bex. "In case the laptop idea failed." She lowered her head and parted her hair. "Take a look."

"It's okay," said Eddie. "We already know you're not a natural green."

"The microchip, you idiot," Bex snorted. "My dad had it attached just before we left for the shuttle. It contains some of *his* mind and connects it directly to mine. Voilà the voice. It also emits a signal that jammed and then temporarily overloaded the computers up here."

"Explaining the very welcome glitch in the countdown," deduced Lori.

"Exactly. And it goes so well with the jewelry, doesn't it?"

"A real chip off the old block," grinned Eddie.

Jake wasn't grinning. Partly, he couldn't help thinking that mind control was still mind control, whatever the intention. And partly it was "Jennifer," he reminded his teammates. "We still have to find her."

"There's got to be some sort of intercom, hasn't there?" Ben queried. "We can just put out an announcement that all is well. Cal?"

Puzzledly. "Hold on, guys. We're getting a signal from the escape pod. I'll put it onscreen."

"Can you not?" Eddie groaned. "I don't think I can take another Frankenstein gloat."

But the Frankenstein who flickered into life on the central viewing screen was not gloating. And there was no need to look any further for Jennifer, either.

"As you were, Dr. Frankenstein," Jennifer commanded coldly, "strapped into your seat. Cuts down on the risk of any sudden moves, you see. Any sudden moves, and this shock blaster I'm holding may just go off. I don't think a cloned stomach is going to stand in its way any more than an original one, do you? Now move."

Frankenstein stole furtive glances to his left and right. Not helpful. Not usually any requirement to escape from an escape pod. He resigned himself to speech: "How resourceful you are, my dear. Of course, I take some credit for that, don't I, as I am, in a sense, your father."

"My father's dead." Jennifer's green eyes were deep and bleak. "So was I." Her expression fixed and determined. "An evil man called Talon killed me. I remember it all. Another evil man brought me back, but you already know about that, don't you,

Dr. Frankenstein? And why are you still on your feet?" She fired the shock blaster at that particular part of the man's anatomy, made him jump backward.

"All right. All right." Frankenstein buckled himself back into his seat. "There. I've done as you wish, my dear, and now I suppose you'll want to return the pod to the Guardian Star and your precocious little group of friends?"

Jennifer nearly laughed then, and the kind of laugh that it nearly was sent a warning chill down Frankenstein's cloned spine. "Return?"

"Way to go, Jen!" Jake was jubilant as Jennifer appeared on the viewing screen. "We should've known you'd be finding yourself something useful to do. The bad guy all tied up like a Christmas turkey." He nudged Eddie and Bex, who were standing nearest, in a that's-my-girl kind of way. "So are you turning that thing around or are we going to have to wait until we've all got our feet on solid ground again?"

Lori was looking at Jennifer closely, didn't like what she saw. In her eyes, an emptiness, a distance like she was already too far away from them to come back. Lori felt a sudden ache in her own heart. What Jennifer went on to say did not surprise her.

"Jake, will you just listen? There's something I need to tell you, all of you, and there's not much time before we hit the atmosphere."

"Before . . .?" Jake's smile froze on his face.

"You've got to help me!" Frankenstein pleaded from his chair. "Do something! She's gone mad! Her mind . . . she means to kill us both!"

"Shut up, Frankenstein," said Jennifer levelly, "or your

mouth will have company." She wafted the shock blaster toward his perspiring forehead.

"What's he talking about, Jen?" Jake seemed drawn toward the screen, mesmerized by it.

"Jake, I remember everything now. Being with you in LA to avenge my parents. Kim leading me into a trap. I should have waited for you, shouldn't I? Maybe things might have been different if I'd waited, but I was too . . . emotional. That was stupid. But I paid for it, didn't I?"

The others were transfixed by Jennifer's speech, but Lori was at Cally's side. "Cal, we've got to get Jennifer back here before . . . well, like *now*. Can you override the pod's system or something?"

Cally shook her head helplessly. "The escape pod's independent and self-sustaining. That's the point."

"Talon killed me, didn't he, and I suppose I ought to want to know what happened to him then, whether you avenged me —"

"He's dead," Jake said. "Jen, all that's over with."

"— but it seems so irrelevant now." She sighed deeply. "I'm not really Jennifer Chen at all, am I? I'm a clone, a copy, a pawn in Frankenstein's plans against you. And I know what happens to clones in the end. I saw Grant's melt. I'm not going to let that happen to me."

"It won't need to!" Jake was crying. "The medics at Spy High, they won't let it. Don't give up, Jen! You've got to come back to us! Cally, don't just sit there. Get a tractor beam or something. Bex, get your dad to jam the pod's systems or I don't know . . ."

"It's too far, Jake," Bex said sadly.

"Jake, listen to me." Jennifer again. "I know this is going to be difficult for you, but you have to understand, for me it's easy, an easy choice to make. My life is a lie. This body is a lie. I died, Jake, and that was it. Cloning me was wrong. I don't want to be a freak, a monster. I want to be remembered for what I did and who I *really* was. I want you to remember me in those ways."

"Jen, this is madness! You can't do this!"

Jennifer closed her eyes. "I can. It's all I can do."

"Don't just stand there gawking!" Frankenstein was still bleating. "You're supposed to be secret agents. Act like it. Save me!"

"We're approaching Earth's atmosphere," Jennifer said. "I'm going to lower the heat shields. It'll be painless and quick, and I doubt Dr. Frankenstein will give you any more trouble." The madman's despairing wail suggested not. "So I'm going to end this communication now."

"No, Jen, don't —"

"Good luck. Have a wonderful life, Jake. All of you. Think of me sometimes."

"No, don't turn the —"

But the screen was already blank.

"Insane! This is insane! The last of the Frankensteins can't end like this!"

The temperature inside the escape pod was rising. Earth filled the viewport.

"There's still time! Raise the heat shields, Jennifer. Do it! We can still live!"

"Live?" mused Jennifer Chen. "We both stopped living a long time ago. It's too late for that, Frankenstein. It's too late for everything."

The hull began to glow, began to smoke. The warning lights flashed in vain.

When the end came, she welcomed it.

There was silence in the control center. Even the sniveling of the president had ceased. The Guardian Star's instruments, the instruments that did not lie, recorded without comment the destruction of the escape pod. It had burned up in the atmosphere. Any life-forms aboard were now extinguished.

Cally hung her head guiltily before the computers. All those switches, all that technology, and nothing had been of any use. Eddie had fallen quiet, for the loss of a teammate was no time for jokes. He seemed unaware of Bex by his side. Ben glanced at Corporal Keene as if to take his lead from the teacher, but the man's face was impassive. He looked instead to Jake, whose legs seemed to have crumbled like dust and who was hunched on the floor with no strength or will to move.

"Not again," Jake was mumbling. "I can't have lost her again."

Maybe Ben should go over to him, offer condolences and sympathy stuff, only it hadn't gone down too well last time, and besides, someone else was there first. Ben turned away, and his hurt was no longer just because of Jennifer.

A hand rested on Jake's shoulder, gently, understandingly. He gazed up to see whose hand it was.

Lori Angel.

EPILOGUE

Blue sky. Blue sea. Yellow sun and sand.

"Guess if paradise had a color, this'd be it," said Bex Deveraux, slowly scanning the shoreline and the glittering ocean beyond. "Blue and yellow, I mean. Plus maybe green for the palm trees."

"I don't know," considered Eddie alongside her. "I think black and purple come close."

Bex looked quizzical until she remembered the colors of her bikini. "Yeah? Well you haven't reached paradise yet, buster, and if you don't put that tongue away, you're gonna dehydrate. No, I think I'll stick with blue and yellow. Might even dye the hair like that, in stripes, maybe. What do you think?"

"Won't the dye affect that chip your dad put in?"

"Not likely, Eddie," Bex said, "seeing as Dad's taken it out again." She cast her eyes farther along the beach to where the rest of Bond Team sat on towels. The Coral Island program was supposed to help them relax, but only Cally appeared to be actively sunbathing. Jake, Lori, and Ben looked like they were attending a conference in advanced philosophy, deep in thought, occasionally glancing at one another as if expecting someone to say something of profound importance but always being disappointed. Gnawed lips and chins rested glumly on hands. No communication. If there was a chill in this virtual Caribbean, it emanated from the three of them. Bex observed it all and sighed. "If only everything else about the mission could be put behind us so easily."

Eddie shrugged. "They'll be okay. We all will. I guess this is what life at Spy High is always going to be like."

"So I'm learning."

"Every day's a danger, but I couldn't possibly leave here now, Bex, could you? And lose that buzz? I mean, think about what we've done. Saved the world from missile attack, put an end to Frankenstein's mad plans, returned the president to the Oval Office —"

"Yeah, well every silver lining's got a cloud."

"— and there's still six weeks of term before Christmas. Who knows what's going to happen in that time?" Carried away by his enthusiasm, Eddie slipped his arm around Bex's shoulders.

"I know one thing that's not." Slipping her shoulders out again.

Eddie continued unabated. "And here we are on this glorious beach in this glorious sunshine while in the real world it's probably freezing cold or raining. What can possibly spoil things now?"

The nearby air quivered, and not with heat haze.

"You had to ask," muttered Bex.

"Still here?" barked an outraged Corporal Keene, thankfully *not* materializing in whatever qualified as a military version of a swimsuit. "You kids think Deveraux's a vacation resort or something?"

"No, sir, Corporal Keene, sir." A uniform chorus, Bond Team snapping to attention along the beach.

"This session should have finished an hour ago. Transfer back to your cyber-cradles at once. You're supposed to be Spy High students, remember? You've got work to do!"

"Ah, well," sighed Eddie, "here we go again . . ."

Turn the page for a sneak peek at

SPY HIGH: MISSION FIVE

BLOOD RELATIONS

Arriving Spring 2005 from
Little, Brown and Company

At the cliff's edge they stopped, where the land seemed to have been torn away like a piece of paper. The ocean was a long way down to a young boy's eyes.

"I thought it was time we had a talk," said Uncle Alex, smiling at him and ruffling his blond hair.

"Yes, Uncle Alex," Ben replied obediently. It always made him feel special when his uncle chose to speak to him, singled out and privileged. He gazed up at the wise, handsome features, the hair prematurely flecked with dignified gray, the eyes that blazed blue and never seemed to blink, the wide and generous smile. When he grew up, he wanted to be Uncle Alex.

"What do you see, Ben?" The man pointed out beyond the headland. "Tell me what you see."

Ben's lower lip quivered. He couldn't see anything. It seemed to him that Uncle Alex's finger was pointing nowhere. But he had to give the right answer, had to. He couldn't let Uncle Alex down, not now that he was six. But he couldn't lie, either. "I don't . . . I don't . . ."

"The sky, Ben," said Uncle Alex gently. "You see the sky, don't you?" Ben nodded eagerly. Of course he saw the sky. "Good. Very Good. And do you know what the sky stands for, Ben?"

This question seemed impenetrable to Ben, but he was going to hazard a guess at "daytime" before Uncle Alex supplied his own answer, almost as if he'd never expected Ben to try in the first place.

"It stands for dreams," he said. "It stands for ambition. Do you know what ambition is, Ben?"

"Something you've always wanted to do." He knew that one all right, the words tumbling out and almost tripping over each other in their haste.

"Good boy," Uncle Alex approved, and Ben flushed proudly. "And ambition is very important. Everyone has to have an ambition, a desire, something to give their lives meaning. Everyone needs to reach out to touch the sky. That's what I've brought you here to tell you, Ben. I think you're old enough to know on your birthday. You must have ambitions, too."

"Yes, Uncle Alex." As many as you want, Ben thought.

"Because we are special people, Ben, your family, mine, others like us. You'll come to understand that as you grow older. We have been chosen to be great. We have been born to lead. What we own and what we are mean that there is nothing we cannot accomplish in our lives, nothing we cannot achieve." Ben felt a strange excitement in him that was almost like tears. Uncle Alex filled his vision like the world. "But we have to have courage. We have to have strength. We have to believe in ourselves."

"Yes, Uncle Alex." Courage. Strength. Belief.

"Because if we do . . . what is there between us and the sky, Ben?"

"Nothing, Uncle Alex."

"Excellent. Excellent indeed. Nothing," the man repeated.

And he jumped off the cliff.